Dust

By S. E. Smith

Acknowledgments

I would like to thank my husband Steve for believing in me and being proud enough of me to give me the courage to follow my dream. I would also like to give a special thank-you to Sally, Debbie, Julie, Jolanda and Narelle, who listen to me, read my stories, and encourage me to be me.

—S. E. Smith

Montana Publishing
Young Adult
DUST: Before and After

First E-Book Published March 2016
Cover Design by Melody Simmons

Summary: A teenage boy wakes to a different world after a comet hits Earth only to discover he has changed, and so have some of the other creatures on the planet.

ISBN: 978-1-942562-84-9 (Paperback)
ISBN: 978-1-942562-83-2 (eBook)

Published in the United States by Montana Publishing.

{1. Post Apocalyptic – Fiction. 2. Science Fiction – Fiction. 3. Paranormal – Fiction. 4. Young Adult – Fiction. – 5. Romance – 6. Horror}

www.montanapublishinghouse.com

Synopsis

Dust wakes to discover the world as he knew it is gone after fragments of a comet hit the Earth. It isn't the only thing that has changed, though, so has Dust. He now possesses powers that continue to grow, but also come with a price. A deadly encounter after he leaves his home leads to a new discovery, – other survivors.

Dust soon learns that another creature has risen from the ashes, one that is determined to possess the powers that he has. On a journey filled with danger, it will take the skills of not just Dust, but those of his friends, if they are to survive.

This time the race is not to the swift, but to the deadliest in a world where a changed human boy and an odd assortment of friends must face their worst nightmares, and accept that life on Earth will never be the same again.

Join Dust and his friends as they fight to overcome an evil force determined to create a new species unlike anything the world has ever known.

Contents

Chapter 1

Before and After:

Dust woke from his sleep, blinking up at the dark gray skies. He could see the swirl of acidic clouds through the hole in the ceiling. It took a moment for his body to catch up with his mind.

He often forgot to focus on it. Since the morning he woke up alone in a collapsed building that had once been his home, he realized that things would never be the same. Before, he was just a fourteen year old boy who loved playing video games and hated going to school. A year had passed since the day the comet hit the Earth. A year since the strange cloud had washed through the small town where he had lived *Before*. That is what he called his life... Before. Now, he was in the After.

His body wrenched as it came back to its solid form. He was used to the feeling now and thought no more about his unusual ability to dissolve into the shadows. Rising up off the floor, he stretched and twisted. Glancing around, he walked over to the bent metal cabinet where he had hidden his knapsack. It contained one pair of jeans, one shirt, a clean pair of underwear and socks, and a bottle of water.

With a wave of his hand, the debris in front of the cabinet rose up into the air and moved. He opened the door and pulled out the dark green knapsack he had found in one of his many excursions over the past year. Slinging the strap over his shoulder, he turned and quietly left the building.

Dust paused on the sidewalk outside the small convenience store where he had taken refuge. His disheveled brown hair stuck out in all directions. Glancing around, his dark brown eyes paused on a moving shadow between two abandoned cars halfway down the street. The sense of danger rose in his gut. His gaze narrowed on the three shadowy forms that slowly stepped out from between them.

Devil dogs.

He didn't know if that was what they were really called, but that was the name he had given them. They were like him... different.

Turning, he slipped the straps over his shoulders so he could run faster. It was time to move on. Where there were three of the creatures, there could be more. Dust felt the adrenaline surge through him as he took off at a steady pace, glancing back and forth as he ran through the center of the small town he had arrived in late the night before. He had hoped to find food. The changes to his body demanded that he eat more often.

Food wasn't always the easiest thing to find. The lack of it was what had finally forced him to leave the small town where he had lived with his family during the time Before. As the sole survivor, he had foraged for every piece of food he could find during the past year until he could find no more.

Dust didn't bother turning to see where the creatures were. He knew they would follow him. They were hungry. He knew, because he felt the same hunger. There would be a fight, of that he had no doubt. Up ahead was the shell of a two-story building. With a wave of his hand, the door was ripped off its hinges and it flew out behind him. He heard a snarl and a thud. They were closer than he'd realized.

Sprinting across the sidewalk, he disappeared into the shadows and allowed his body to dissolve. It would be difficult to keep his shadow form for long. He desperately needed food if he was going to continue using the amount of energy that he needed to maintain this form. Scooping up a metal pipe as he flew by, he turned just as the first shape came through the door behind him. The end of the pipe caught the creature in the chest, impaling it and driving him back against the wall. His body solidified at the force and the wind was knocked from him as he slammed into the wall.

The creature's glowing red eyes flashed and its jaws snapped, but he could already see the light fading. He immediately recognized that the creatures must be starving to attack him so boldly. Not only that, they couldn't hold their shadow form any longer than he could. He pressed the metal rod down to the floor and forced the metal tip further through the beast and twisted it. The creature's loud snarls turned to a scream before silence engulfed the room. Dust didn't wait. There were at least two left, possibly more.

Ripping the pipe out of the creature, he turned toward the open stairwell. The faint sound of glass crunching under heavy feet pulled his gaze to the ceiling. He could hear one of them. It must have gone through an upper level window. Dust's jaw tightened. He would have to kill all of them or the creatures would follow him and he would never find food or rest. His fingers wrapped around the cool metal and he started up the steps, taking them in a slow, steady climb. He was almost to the top when the huge black creature appeared at the top of the stairs.

Dust glanced over his shoulder when he heard a second snarl behind him. He was stuck between the two beasts. Glancing back and forth, he realized that they had set up a trap for him. A shiver ran through him. He started when the one above him suddenly jumped. Focusing, he used more of his precious energy. The creature flashed through his body, sending a wave of nausea through him. His body once more solidified and he thrust upward, pushing the rod through its soft underbelly while it was still in the air. He allowed the weight of the creature to twist him around. The force of the movement and his gradually weakening strength tore the metal pipe from his hands as it crashed into the beast moving up the stairs at the same time.

Stumbling back against the wall, he watched as the dying creature struck its companion. He gripped the stairwell and pulled himself up. He needed to find another weapon before the last beast regained his footing. His legs shook as he half crawled, half climbed the stairs. He barely had time to roll to the side before the third creature came up through the narrow opening and turned. Dust rolled to his stomach, his gaze froze on the heaving chest and foaming jaws. His arms trembled and he knew he didn't have the strength to dissolve.

He pushed upward in a slow, steady movement, never taking his eyes off the beast. He was almost to his feet when it sprang. Jumping, he twisted to the side and rolled. Almost immediately he was back on his feet and twisting around. The beast had slid into a large wooden desk. The force of its body hitting the desk shattered one of the legs and the heavy piece of furniture collapsed on top of it. He took advantage of the reprieve, darting down the staircase. He jumped over the dead creature at the bottom, tearing out the metal pipe protruding from its chest. Running, he burst back outside.

A loud crash resounded behind him. Dust didn't pause. Spying an abandoned SUV with its door partially open across the street, he pushed every ounce of energy he had left inside him to his quivering legs. He reached out and grabbed the door handle, pulling it open far enough to squeeze through. He barely had time to pull it closed before the beast hit the door with enough force to knock the SUV onto two wheels. The force of the blow knocked Dust across the console and into the passenger seat.

He quickly pulled his legs up when the glass on the driver's door shattered.

Dust fumbled for the handle behind him as the beast thrust its long black head inside, its jaws snapping viciously at his legs. Blood dripped on the fine leather interior from where the ragged glass cut into the beast's neck. That didn't stop it. If anything, the creature became more enraged, clawing at the glass and pulling it away so it could try to wiggle into the vehicle. Dust kicked out, striking the canine-like snout. It jerked its head back, giving him just enough room to grab the door handle. He fell out the other side, landing heavily on his back. Kicking his foot out again, he slammed the door just as the creature jumped into the driver's seat.

Rolling stiffly onto his hands and knees, he gripped the metal rod in his hand and rose to his feet. Glancing back at the snarling beast, he took off running. It was only a matter of seconds before he heard the sound of breaking glass again. Ducking under a torn awning, he darted through the open door of another building. It didn't take long for him to realize his mistake. The back section of the building was blocked by fallen debris. The only thing separating him from death was a tall refrigerated display case and the metal pipe in his hand. Turning, he backed up as the dark shadow paused in the entrance.

"Don't move until I tell you," a soft voice said behind him.

Chapter 2

Someone else lives:

Dust froze, his eyes locked on the blazing red eyes of the devil dog even as he wanted to turn to the sound of the voice. It was the first voice other than his own that he'd heard in over a year. Afraid he was dreaming, he stood ready, holding the bloody pipe in front of him.

The beast took another step and snarled. White foam dripped from its mouth and its yellow teeth snapped as it moved through the doorway. Dust knew it was about to attack. The sound of the voice yelling for him to move echoed through the air at the same time as a thin shaft flew past his right shoulder.

He jumped to the side, sliding under a table that was bolted to the floor. His back hit the wall and he jerked his legs out of the way as the beast's thick, black body slid across the few feet of cleared space on the dirty tile. He stared in shock at the two thick shafts of wood sticking out of its throat and upper chest. The beast's red eyes were blank and its jaw hung open as it pulled in its last breath of air.

Dust slowly scooted out from under the table, keeping his eyes on the creature just in case. He was rising to his feet when a movement behind the counter caught his attention. Turning, he held the dark gray pipe out in front of him. Two figures, one slightly taller than the other rose from behind an old display. Swallowing, Dust stared at the two dirty faces looking back at him with a combination of curiosity and fear. It took a moment for him to realize that the tall person was pointing one of the long arrows at him.

Dust waited, staring at the girl. He saw her swallow, but she didn't lower the bow in her hands. The small boy next to her scooted slightly behind her when Dust glanced at him. His gaze returned to the girl's face. He curled his fingers into a tight fist as a wave of dizziness washed through him. The hunger was beginning to become unbearable. He needed something to eat.

"Who are you?" Dust asked in a rusty voice, his eyes locked on the face of the young girl who seemed to be close to his own age.

Dust swayed as he waited for the girl to respond. He saw her swallow again and nervously bite her bottom lip. She still didn't lower the bow in her hands, even though he had dropped the pipe to his side. The small boy next to her stared back at Dust with a wide-eyed, curious expression. Dust kept his gaze fixed on the girl's face.

"Who are you?" The girl suddenly demanded, staring at him through narrow eyes.

Dust flexed the fingers of his right hand, trying to stay focused. "Dust," he said in a low, hoarse voice.

"Sammy, he don't look so good," the boy whispered, tugging on her shirt.

"What's wrong with you?" Sammy asked in a tight voice.

"Food," Dust whispered, uncurling the fingers of his left hand and letting the pipe drop to the floor with a loud thump. He felt his legs begin to shake so much that he couldn't hold himself up. "I need food."

The girl lowered the bow when his knees gave out on him and he sank to the floor. His head fell forward and he drew in a deep breath before gagging when the stench of the dead devil dog poured through his nose. Shaking his head, he closed his eyes and shakily lifted his arm to cover his nose.

"We need to get out of here," the girl said in a soft voice, stepping around the edge of the display case. "Todd, get me one of the bars."

"But, Sammy," Todd protested. "We don't have but three left."

Sammy frowned at the small boy that appeared to be around seven years old. "Now we have two," she stated, holding out her hand. "Get me one of them."

Dust didn't bother opening his eyes. He was afraid if he did that the two of them would disappear. Instead, he rested his cheek against his bent arm.

"Here," Sammy said. "Eat this, but do it slow so you don't get sick."

Dust lifted his head and opened his eyes. Sammy was holding out a small fruit bar. His mouth watered and he reached shakily for it. Their fingers touched for a brief moment and he almost jerked back. He could tell she was just as surprised as he was at the contact. Taking the small bar of food from her hand, he nodded his thanks before lifting it to his mouth and taking a bite.

All too soon, it was gone. His eyes closed again for a moment as he felt a surge of energy. It wouldn't last long, but it was enough to keep him going. His eyes popped open when he felt the tentative touch on his arm again.

"We really need to get going," Sammy said, rising to her feet and holding her hand out. "I don't know how many more of those creatures there are. I counted four earlier."

Dust nodded, reaching up and gripping her hand. He rose clumsily to his feet before bending down and picking up the bloody metal pipe. Testing it, he glanced at Sammy and Todd.

"I killed two of them. This makes three," he muttered, staring out the doorway. "I need more food."

"There's a small grocery store at the end of the street," Sammy said, uneasily. "That's where we were headed when we saw those things and hid in here. It's just a few doors down."

Dust lifted his arm, stopping Sammy when she started to walk around him. His gaze flickered from her to Todd and back again. If there was still another one of those creatures out there, he would go first.

"I'll go first, you follow," he said in a rough voice. "Keep the kid between us."

"I know how to take care of us," Sammy muttered, glancing at Todd. "Hand me the backpack, Todd."

"I've got it, Sammy," Todd mumbled. "You need your hands free."

Dust felt a tug of emotion when Sammy smiled tenderly down at the boy. For a moment, he felt a wave of envy. There were times in the past year that he would have given anything to have someone to talk to. He drew in a deep breath, now wasn't the time to think of the past. He needed to find more food before the little bit of strength he had deserted him.

Grabbing a hold of the door frame, he glanced outside. His gaze carefully moved down along the street in both directions before pausing on the building across the street. If there were only four of the devil dogs, then they should be okay. He could kill the other one. He glanced over his shoulder and jerked his head to Sammy and Todd. Stepping outside, he walked slowly down the sidewalk along the buildings, pausing every once in a while to search the shadows.

A sigh of relief poured through Dust when he saw the sign for the small grocery store hanging at an odd angle. He really hoped there was still some food inside. His steps increased as they drew nearer. He was passing a small barber shop when a movement inside caught his attention. The shadowy form exploded through the plate glass window just as he turned.

The devil dog's snapping jaws barely missed his throat as it hit him in the chest. The only thing that saved him was the metal pipe he had raised and gripped between both of his hands. A grunt of pain escaped him when the creature's sharp claws sliced through his thin shirt and across his chest. Twisting, he tripped on the edge of the curb and landed heavily on his back in the road.

Dust jerked his head back when the beast lunged again for his neck. His arms strained to keep it back, but its front and back legs were cutting through his clothing. A hoarse yell escaped him when the beast suddenly yelped and rolled away from him. He turned onto his side, staring at it as it wobbled for a moment before it turned and half ran, half limped away, the shaft of one of Sammy's arrows sticking out of its front shoulder.

"You're bleeding," Sammy said, kneeling down beside him. "Did it bite you?"

Dust shook his head and grimaced as the pain from the numerous cuts flashed through him. "No, just scratches," he muttered, leaning on the pipe as Sammy slid her arm around his waist.

"I'll lead," she said, turning to Todd. "You help him."

Todd just nodded. His eyes were wide with fear. He stepped forward and stood next to Dust.

"What if there's more?" Todd whispered, glancing back at where the devil dog had disappeared between two buildings.

"Then we'll deal with them," Sammy said, fitting her last arrow into the bow. "I need to either get the arrows I shot or find more."

"I need food first," Dust muttered, beginning to droop again. "Food, then we'll look."

"Hopefully there are some medical supplies there as well," Sammy said with a worried glance at the blood coating the front of Dust's shredded shirt. "Let's go."

Dust just nodded. Once he had food in his system, it wouldn't take long for his skin to heal. It was one of the things he had learned after he had awoken from the change. Gritting his teeth against the pain, he leaned against Todd so he wouldn't fall flat on his face again. They stepped back up onto the sidewalk and continued the few feet to the entrance of the store.

The large front window and the glass in the front doors were shattered. Sammy lowered her bow and peered through the opening before reaching over and tugging the door open. The loud screeching sound of metal hitting the glass as it pushed against the concrete drew a wince from all of them. Sammy glanced back at Todd and Dust before squaring her shoulders and stepping through into the dark interior.

Chapter 3

The Search for Food:

She and Todd hadn't known what was going on that day almost a year ago. Her dad had been at work and her mom had driven into town for a doctor's appointment. She had been watching Todd when the weather alert went off. At first, she thought it was a mistake because the skies had been a crystal clear blue, but the alert said that it wasn't and that emergency precautions needed to be made. She had dragged Todd down into the storm cellar buried out behind the house.

They were almost there when they saw the huge, dark cloud rolling toward them. Sammy had never seen anything like it. Frightened, she had ordered Todd to get down behind the boxes in the back as she slammed the door shut and locked it. Seconds later, the light on the inside had gone out and the entire shelter had shaken so hard that Sammy had been thrown to the floor.

The aftershocks continued for days and the sound of dirt and rocks hitting the door had lasted even longer. For a while, Sammy had actually feared that they might get buried under the onslaught. When it finally stopped, they had waited... and waited... and waited for either their mom or dad to come tell them that it was safe to come out. Sammy had used the flashlights stored in the shelter sparingly. Fortunately, the growing season had just ended and the huge collection of canned goods she and her mom had processed and stored for selling remained protected from the fallout.

A week had gone by before Sammy finally worked at forcing the door to the shelter open. The land around the house was barren, stripped clear by the blast. Only the shell of their house and the barn remained. She and Todd had searched the area, but they seemed to be the only ones left alive. Remembering her father's warning that if there was ever an emergency to stay put until someone came for them, Sammy salvaged what she could from the ruins of the house and returned to the storm shelter.

They had waited for someone to come, but no one ever did. When the food started to get low, she and Todd began venturing to neighboring farms in the hope they would find someone. They discovered the occasional can of food, but never another living human soul.

The first strange creature they discovered had been small. She and Todd were on their way back to the shelter from a neighboring farm. They had stopped at a narrow bridge over a dried creek to rest. The thing had come up from under the bridge and grabbed Todd's pant leg. She used a long walking stick that she had found and beat the thing to death. They had run back to the shelter and hidden for two days.

It had taken her a while to finally understand that the thing had been some type of mutated animal. That was when she searched the barn for her dad's old bow and arrows that he used when he went hunting. She spent hour after hour each day practicing until she was confident she could protect herself and Todd if need be. Two months later, their food was dangerously low and she knew they had no choice but to leave the shelter and search for some - and more survivors.

"I see food," she said, shaking away the memories as she stepped through the doorway. "It looks like the creatures didn't get all of it, only the stuff they could reach and open."

"I... I just need something... anything... for now," Dust muttered in a voice filled with pain.

Sammy glanced at the bent shelf that was closer to her. There were cans of green beans on it. It would have to do. Gripping the bow in her right hand, she walked over to the shelf and grabbed a can. She turned and wove her way along the row of cash registers, searching for something to open the can with, when she saw a can opener hanging from the tab along with other items. Grabbing it, she quickly removed the top of the can before turning to walk over to where Dust was sinking down next to a pile of shredded candy wrappers. She held the can of green beans out to him.

"Be careful, the edge is sharp," she said. "I'll go look for some medical supplies. Todd, you start picking up as many cans of food as you can and stack them near Dust. We'll figure out what to do with them once we have an idea of how much there is."

"Okay," Todd said, sliding the backpack off his thin shoulders.

Sammy glanced one last time toward Dust where he sat frantically eating the green beans, liquid and all. Her gaze flashed over his chest. She'd have to see if there were any clothes along with the medical supplies. She reached down next to him and picked up one of the handheld shopping baskets before turning to walk away.

She glanced up at the signs above each aisle. Number ten held cosmetics and bandages. She carefully walked down the center aisle, pausing to glance down each row as she went. It looked like most of the items had been either knocked off the shelves or crushed.

Turning down aisle number ten, she quickly grabbed everything she could off the shelves. Once the basket was filled, she released a frustrated groan. She would need to get more baskets. Food and medical supplies were essential. How they would carry everything, she didn't know, but for now, she wasn't going to worry about it. Remembering the blood covering Dust, she turned and hurried back down the aisle to where she had left him.

"I found some...," Sammy's voice died when she saw the four empty cans of green beans next to Dust. That wasn't what froze the words in her throat. "What happened...? How did...? What are you?" She asked in a trembling voice, staring at his chest.

Sammy's fingers instinctively searched for the bow she always carried. A curse swept through her mind when she remembered that she had set it down to gather the medical supplies. Swallowing, she dropped the basket in her hand and took a step back as Dust rose to his feet. Her eyes remained glued to his chest. There was dried blood on his skin where the devil dog had clawed him. The front of his shredded T-shirt was proof that she hadn't imagined the attack a short while ago. Only now, instead of ripped flesh there was smooth, unmarred skin.

"I don't know," Dust replied, staring back at her with an intense expression on his face. "But, I know that I won't hurt you or Todd."

Sammy shook her head, her eyes flashing from his face to his chest. She bit her lip, trying to decide if she should scream for Todd to run or stand her ground. Her gaze flickered to the front door. If they ran, how far could they get? That thing was still out there and they needed food. She was also out of arrows. In here... There was food, medicine, and... Dust. Swallowing, she locked gazes with Dust again. Could she trust him? That was the real question.

Chapter 4

What is he?

Dust stared at the two figures walking ahead of him. He glanced down and kicked at a stone in the road when Sammy looked over her shoulder at him again. A small smile tugged at the corner of his mouth. She had been glaring at him for the past two hours. At first, she had backed away from him. When it became obvious that he wasn't going to attack her and Todd, she had tried ignoring him. They had worked quietly gathering as much food as they could and placing it in stacks.

He found some more shirts on one of the aisles and quickly changed out of his torn and bloody one. He had also snacked on anything he could find and felt better than he had in ages. He paused when she stopped to stare inside one of the small cars left in the middle of the road. Curious, she opened the door and slid into the driver's seat. He jumped when he heard the clicking of the engine. His expression softened when Sammy leaned her forehead against the steering wheel.

"Pop the hood," he called out.

Sammy slowly lifted her head and stared at him in silence before she bent down and pulled the lever. Dust stepped forward and felt under the hood until he found the latch. Pulling it, he lifted the hood and pulled the thin bar down to hold it up. He glanced around the engine, looking for anything obvious.

"Can you fix it?" Todd asked, coming up to stand next to Dust.

"Maybe," Dust replied, touching some of the wires and hoses, before checking the battery. "Does it have any gas?"

Sammy stepped up to look up under the hood. "I don't know," she said with a shrug. "The battery is dead."

Dust grinned. "I might be able to help with that," he commented, looking around. "Wait here."

***

"Where else are we going to go?" Sammy muttered under her breath as she turned to watch him jog across the street. "Shit!"

"Sammy!" Todd exclaimed, watching Dust with wide eyes.

"Sorry," she muttered, staring at the spot where Dust had just disappeared – literally. "He just went through that door without opening it!"

"I know," Todd whispered in awe. "I wish I could do that!"

Sammy didn't say anything. Instead, she watched as the door opened this time and Dust walked out. He had disappeared inside what looked like a discount auto store. He had several things in a dark red basket. He stopped in front of the car and set the basket down before rubbing his hands nervously down the front of his pants.

"I used to help my dad in his shop," Dust admitted. "It may take a little while, but all we've got is time, right?" He joked, looking at Sammy with a slightly pleading look.

"Why are you doing this?" Sammy asked, swallowing over the lump in her throat. "What happened to you?"

Dust bent his head and shook it. "I don't want you to go without me," he said softly. Clearing his throat, he bent and picked up the tools he had picked out and set them on the edge of the radiator. "You two are the first humans that I've seen in over a year. The only other thing I've seen are a few animals and…."

"And?" Sammy asked, motioning for Todd to take the pack in her hands. "Can you put this in the car."

"Okay. Can I help you, Dust?" Todd asked with a hopeful smile.

Dust nodded. "Sure," he said. "Can you make sure everything is cleaned out as much as possible so we can load the car up when we get it going?"

Todd's face fell, but he nodded his head and kicked at a loose rock. "Yeah, I guess," he mumbled.

"If I need more help, I'll call you," Dust promised. "This is important, though. We've got to have supplies."

"That's okay," Todd replied with a hesitant smile. "Can you teach me how to go through doors like you did?"

Dust's smile faded and he bowed his head again. Sammy shook her head at Todd, who released a loud sigh and turned away. Sammy's gaze followed her little brother with a look of worry.

"I won't hurt him… or you," Dust muttered. "You asked me what happened to me. I don't know," he said, bending forward and beginning to pull the spark plugs. Both the plugs and wires were scorched. He quickly removed them and tossed them to the side. "I don't remember much after the initial blast. I was in the house alone. My mom and dad were in the barn, trying to bring the cows inside."

"What… What happened to them?" Sammy asked, watching as Dust worked.

Dust glanced at her before bending to pick up some new spark plugs he had taken from the auto store. Sammy wished she could take back the question, but it was too late. Dust turned away from her and worked in silence for several minutes before he spoke again.

"They were gone and so was the barn. There wasn't much left of the house," he said in a low voice. "I woke up buried in the cellar. I could see through the roof. I remember a strange light in the sky, bolts of lightning striking all around me and a strange dust. It all mixed together and everything began to glow. The next time I woke, I was…."

"You were…," Sammy prompted, placing her hand lightly on his arm before jerking it away.

Dust's head slowly turned and he looked at her with piercing brown eyes. "I was there, but I wasn't."

Sammy stared at him for a long time before she nodded, as if she had made up her mind about something. Biting her lip, she looked at where Todd was playing. Her heart hurt for both Todd and Dust. Life shouldn't be like this. Blinking back the tears, she looked back at Dust and blushed a little when she saw he was watching her.

"Todd can stay here and help you," she said suddenly. "I'll start bringing stuff from the store and packing it into the car. This way we can get out of here as soon as you get it started."

"Okay," Dust replied, glancing back down the street with a frown. "Be careful. We don't know what happened to that one devil dog and we don't know if there are more."

"I will be," Sammy said, stepping back. "Just… Promise me that you'll keep Todd safe."

Dust straightened. "I promise," he replied. "I'll keep you both safe – or die trying."

"Let's hope that won't be necessary," Sammy retorted with an unsteady laugh, pushing her hair back behind her ear.

"Take your bow," Dust advised.

Sammy shook her head. "I only have one arrow left. I'll borrow your pipe," she said, reaching for the long piece of metal leaning up against the front of the car. "Just get the car going."

Sammy didn't wait for Dust to reply. Instead, she focused on the task she had assigned herself. If Dust was successful, she wanted to get out of here. Her gut was telling her that they didn't want to be here after dark tonight.

Chapter 5

A Way Out:

Dust listened to Todd as he ran around the car. Glancing at the boy, he made sure that he couldn't see what he was about to do. The battery was dead and there was no way to jump it.

Checking on Todd once more, he held his hands above the battery where the cables connected. A burst of energy shot out from the palm of his hand. He kept it that way for a moment before he pulled his hand back.

He wiped his hands on the cloth he had found in the store and walked around to the driver's side. Sliding in, he turned the key. The engine tried to turn over, but couldn't quite make it. Fortunately, the gauges were now working and he could see that the car had an almost full tank of gas. Turning the key off, he slid back out of the car and looked for Todd.

"Todd, I need your help, dude," Dust called.

Todd's head whipped around and a huge smile lit his face. He dropped the stick he was playing with and ran over to Dust. Dust couldn't help but grin at the boy's enthusiasm.

"What'cha need help with?" Todd asked excitedly.

Dust nodded to the driver's seat. "I need you to turn the key when I tell you to," he said. "Do you know how?"

"Sure, my dad would let me start the truck if it was cold out so it could warm up," Todd replied, sliding into the seat. "Do you need me to give it gas?"

"Not unless I tell you," Dust replied. "I don't want to take a chance of flooding it. I'm not sure how good the gas is, hopefully it isn't too bad."

"Okay, just tell me when," Todd answered with a grin.

Dust walked back around to the front and bent over the battery again. This time, he sent a stronger charge into it and yelled for Todd to try to start it. It took three tries before the car started. It idled roughly at first, but soon smoothed out.

"Just let it idle for a while to give the battery a chance to charge," Dust instructed, turning when he heard the sound of wheels on concrete.

"Wow! That's a great idea, Sammy," Todd said, watching as his sister pushed one shopping cart full of food and items they had salvaged and pulled another one. "Do you want some help?"

Sammy nodded, pushing her hair back from her flushed cheeks. "If you can start packing this in the car, I'll go back for more. There isn't much, but maybe we can find more in another town," she said, turning to look at Dust with delight. "You got it running!"

Dust grinned and polished his fingernails on the front of his shirt. "Of course," he replied with a grin. "I'd like to see if I can find extra gas to take with us, just in case."

"Okay, but that means less for us to pack in the car," Sammy said, looking at the shopping carts.

"No, I'll tie them to the luggage rack," Dust said with a shake of his head. "We can't put the gas in the car. It wouldn't be safe."

"Oh, right," Sammy said with a slight blush. "I knew that."

"I helped Dust start the car, Sammy," Todd boasted. "I'll take care of this stuff while you and Dust get the other stuff."

"Thanks, Todd," Sammy said with an affectionate smile. "One more trip should do it."

"I saw some gas cans in the auto supply store. I'll grab them and anything else I think we could use and meet you back here. I've got to change a couple of the tires, too," Dust explained. He decided he'd better test the engine by turning it off and back on before he left it. He grinned when it started again. Deciding not to waste any more gas than necessary, he shut it back off. "I'll be back in a few minutes. Todd, will you be alright?"

"Sure! If anything comes at me, I'll jump in the car and close the doors," Todd said. "I've done that before."

Dust paused and stared at Todd. "When?" He asked in a tight voice.

"Once on the way here," she said, looking to stare down the road. "There were some other creatures, not as big as the devil dogs, but just like them."

"We saw them attack a stray cow," Todd said in a somber voice. "Sammy and I hid in the car until they were gone. When we finally got out, there wasn't nothing left of the cow, but a few bones."

"They were near the town where we used to live," Sammy said, looking back at Dust. "That's why we came north. We were hoping that they wouldn't be here."

"But they were, just not as many," Todd added.

"How many were there where you were at?" Dust asked, looking at Sammy.

She shrugged and looked down, was silent for a minute before she looked up at him and bit her lip at the dark memory. "I don't know, a dozen or more," she finally said. "It was hard to look and count. They were everywhere and I was afraid they would see us."

Dust's eyes narrowed and he pressed his lips together. A dozen was more than he'd seen at any time. Four, maybe five, but more than a dozen wasn't good. He had noticed back in his home town that they worked together as a pack. It had been difficult, but he had eventually killed the last one. Unfortunately, like him, they needed food, a lot of it to survive and had cleaned out the town fairly quickly. He was surprised that they hadn't done that here. The only reason he could think of was because they hadn't been here for long.

"We'll keep an eye out," he said with a sharp nod. "Todd, pack the car. Sammy, get all the food and supplies that you can. I'll find more gas and anything else I think we might need. How far away is your town from here?"

"Twenty, maybe twenty-five miles or so," Sammy said, pushing her hair behind her ear.

"We need to get out of here," Dust said, turning away. "Something tells me with that many, they are going to be looking for food and traveling fast."

Chapter 6

The Beginning of the Pack:

"That's it," Dust said, pulling on the straps he had found in the auto parts store.

"Dust," Sammy called out suddenly from the other side of the car.

"Yeah?" Dust said, jumping down from where he had been standing on the edge of the open door.

"Look," she murmured, nodding her head. "It's that devil dog I shot with an arrow."

Dust looked at Sammy before turning to see where she was looking. Further down the road, between two abandon vehicles, a dark shadow emerged. He stared at the black beast as it stepped out into the road. He could see the broken shaft of the arrow sticking out of its front shoulder. It looked like it had bitten off the end in an attempt to get it out. Swallowing, he continued to stare at it as he slowly opened the front passenger door.

"Todd, get in the back seat. Sammy, do you know how to drive?" Dust asked, keeping the beast in his view.

"Yes. Well, sort of," she admitted. "My dad used to let me drive the truck on the farm."

"I think now would be a good time to use that skill," Dust said, slamming the back door shut before sliding into the passenger seat. "Go!"

"Sammy, there's more of them!" Todd cried out, looking around as more devil dogs suddenly began to appear.

Dust glanced at Sammy as she slid behind the wheel and slammed the driver's door. Her hand shook as she reached for the key and turned it. He breathed out a sigh of relief when the car started again.

Sammy slammed the gear shift down and pressed her foot on the gas. The car fishtailed as it slipped on the loose gravel in the road and the force of the acceleration. Dust glanced at her face. It was tense, but he saw a focused determination which showed that she was in control. She was leaning forward, staring at the gathering crowd of devil dogs. It would appear that the pack from her and Todd's town had arrived.

"Todd, put your seat belt on," Sammy ordered as the car picked up speed.

Dust braced his hand against the dashboard as Sammy struck the first several creatures. Their massive bodies flew up, shattering the windshield before rolling over the top of the car. He glanced behind them and grimaced when he saw one of the gas cans he had just secured rolling along the road.

"Todd, duck!" Dust ordered, throwing his palm up and sending a bolt of electricity out.

A tiny hole appeared in the back window as the bolt melted the glass. The silvery-white thread struck the gas can. A huge, fiery explosion erupted, sending a shower of burning gas over a number of the creatures that had turned to follow them.

Dust's gaze locked on the lone figure that calmly stepped through the remaining group. It didn't chase them, it just watched with red, glowing eyes. Another creature came up to it and bit down on the broken shaft embedded in its shoulder. With a savage pull, the remains of the arrow were ripped from its body. Within seconds, the creature turned and attacked the one that had helped it.

Dust turned back around in his seat. He pulled the seat belt free and secured it around him. His gaze moved to Sammy. Her lips were pressed into a tight, straight line. He could see her gaze flickering to the rear view mirror before they moved back to the road.

After several long minutes, she finally relaxed a little. Dust watched as she pulled her seat belt over her shoulder and hooked it. He waited, knowing that she wouldn't let go of what had happened.

"When we find a place where it is safe to stop, you have some explaining to do," Sammy finally said.

Dust released a tired breath and nodded. "I figured you'd say that," he mumbled.

Hungry, he reached for a can of peaches in the bag at his feet. Sitting back, he popped the lid and drank the syrup before using his fingers to pull them out. From the look on Sammy's face there was going to be a lot of talking done, primarily by him. He turned when he felt a light tap on his shoulder.

"I thought that was pretty cool," Todd said, glancing at Sammy. "I guess you can't teach me that either, can you?"

Dust chuckled and shook his head. "Probably not," he admitted.

"Ah, well," Todd replied as he sat back in his seat. "It was still cool."

"Thanks," Dust responded with a crooked grin before he glanced at Sammy. "Where to now?"

Sammy frowned and shrugged her shoulders. "I don't know," she said. "See if there are any maps in the glove box. We need to make a plan. Obviously we can't go back the way we came."

Dust licked his fingers and placed the empty can back in the bag before opening the glove box. There were tons of napkins from various fast food restaurants, the car registration, some plastic utensils that he could have used a minute ago, and three straws. Closing it, he sighed. He hadn't thought to check to see if there were any maps in the grocery store or the auto parts place.

"Nothing," he said.

Sammy sighed. "Hopefully the next town we come to won't have those creatures in them and we can find a store that has a map," she replied, glancing at him with unease when she said the word 'creature'.

Dust nodded, trying to ignore the pain caused by her suspicion that he was anything like the devil dogs. Sure, they could do some of the same things, like dissolve. The only difference was he could dissolve all the way and they could only do it a little and for a lot less time. It took a lot of energy to fade, as he thought of the process. Frowning, the only other thing that he knew they could do as well was heal fast, but again, it took a lot of energy to do that which meant they needed food.

He reached for another can of peaches. Opening the can, he drank the juice again, but this time he used one of the plastic forks from the glove box to eat it. Resting his head back against the headrest, he chewed the fruit and wondered what else would happen today.

***

The creature did not understand what was happening to it at first. It had woken with its litter mates under the remains of the house where its mother had given birth to ten puppies. It had staggered out when the rush of ash had fallen and the ground had shaken on trembling legs.

At barely eight weeks old, it was the runt of the litter, but also the most adventuresome. Its mother had tried more than once to keep it hidden from the large, two-legged creatures that walked the ground. That first day, it had fallen, shivering and confused, as strange, green flashes of light mixed with the glowing ash that coated its tiny body.

Its eyes had closed as a strange feeling swept over it. Pain burst through its small body as it grew, twisting and pulling on the bones and tissue until low, whimpering cries were ripped from its throat. When it finally woke several days later, it was hungry. Its mother had come out several times to check on it after the first day, but assumed that it was dead. She returned to the rest of her litter and waited for the world to stop shaking.

It had smelled its mother and siblings hiding under the house. The mother tried to protect her pups, but it had devoured each one before turning its attention to the larger female that it had wounded.

The creature had learned quickly that food gave it the energy it craved. It had learned over the next year how to stalk and kill its prey. There had been other creatures like it, but they had not been as smart.

It recognized that it was different. It was the alpha bitch. She would rule those under her. Only three others had recognized her power and submitted to her dominance. She had allowed them to live, to serve her.

Licking her muzzle clean from the dripping black blood of the beast that ripped the arrow out of her shoulder, she tilted her head and stared at the remaining creatures around her. There were ten of them counting her. Her gaze moved to the ones that were dead or dying. Her pack would need food.

With a low snarl, the others attacked the remains. She bent and ripped another section of black flesh from the beast she had killed. A strange consciousness emerged in her mind. She wanted the powers of the strange two-legged creature and she wanted to kill the female who had challenged her.

But first, first I need food, she thought.

Chapter 7

First Night:

Dust watched Sammy as she peeked in the rear view mirror for the hundredth time to make sure her little brother was alright. The light banter that Todd had kept up turned to a stony silence when he finally fell asleep an hour ago. That silence now sat like an invisible passenger between Dust and Sammy.

Dust stared out the window at the passing scenery, trying to think of something to say. It had grown dark several hours before, so there wasn't much to look at as they were traveling through western Oklahoma.

"The landscape was just rolling hills of nothingness," he muttered under his breath.

"What?" Sammy asked, glancing at him.

Dust turned his head to stare at her in confusion. "Huh?" He asked.

Sammy released a loud breath. "You said something," she retorted. "I didn't hear all of it, just the last word so I asked you 'what' so you would repeat it."

"Oh," Dust replied, not really knowing what else to say. "Um, what word did you hear?"

"Nothingness," Sammy bit out in exasperation.

"Oh," Dust replied again, turning to stare out the window again.

Dust's lips twitched when he heard Sammy mutter a few things about weird boys who didn't finish their sentences or something like that. He turned back to look at her. She was flexing her fingers on the steering wheel.

"Alright, I give up," she finally growled. "What about nothingness?"

Dust shrugged his shoulders. "I was just thinking there is just rolling hills of nothingness out there, is all," he said.

Sammy slowed down when a rabbit darted out across the road. He breathed a sigh of relief when he saw that it was a normal one. A frown creased his brow as he thought about it.

"Where were you...? " He started to say at the same time as she was asking... "How did you...?"

"You go first," Sammy muttered.

"Okay," Dust said. He figured it was better than making her mad again. "Where were you and Todd when the comet hit?

He watched as Sammy blinked rapidly for a moment before she started talking in a quiet voice. She explained how she was home with Todd while her parents had gone to town. The emergency warning system that they had sounded.

"We went to the storm shelter in the backyard," she explained. "Mom and I had just finished canning a bunch of vegetables from the garden. We stored them down there. I saw the cloud heading straight for us. The ground... The ground shook so bad for a while that I thought Todd and I were going to be trapped. We stayed there for as long as we could, waiting for someone to come, but they never did," she whispered. She angrily brushed at her eyes. "It was like everyone was just gone. Your turn," she said in a stronger voice. "How do you do the things you do? You know, like the way you disappear and how you shot that bolt of lightning out of your hand."

"Electricity," Dust corrected before he thought about it. "I guess that's what lightning is, isn't it? I don't know. I remember being in the basement of the house, then everything went black," he murmured, looking out the window. "I woke up a few times. I saw all this dust and strange lights all around me. I remember trying to touch it."

"And," Sammy said when he didn't continue.

Dust shrugged. "I don't remember much after that," he replied in a quiet tone that told her he didn't want to talk about it anymore.

"Well," Sammy finally said with a sigh. "I'm glad you can do whatever it is you can do."

"Including fixing the car?" Dust teased.

"Yeah, well, I would have given you that one if you had remembered to get a map as well," she chuckled. "Talking about cars and maps, we need to find a place to fill up soon. We're getting low and I have to admit, I'm tired."

"Okay," Dust replied, peering down the road.

Twenty minutes later, Sammy pulled into the ghostly remains of a convenience store and pulled to a stop. There wasn't a lot left of it. The roof was torn off, most of one wall was gone, and the awning over the gas pumps was twisted around the few pumps that remained.

"I doubt there is anything left worth looking for," Sammy said with a groan.

"You don't know that," Dust replied, staring at the building. "Why don't we change places? You can put the seat back and I'll keep watch. In the morning, we'll see if there is anything worth salvaging and see if they have any maps. I can also check to see if there is any gas left in the tanks. They were pretty well protected since they are buried."

Sammy reached for the key and turned the car off with a tired yawn. Twisting the knob for the headlights, she turned them off. She really hoped that the car started again in the morning. Another huge yawn escaped her.

"Wake me if you need anything," she mumbled, reaching for the door handle.

"Wait," Dust said, grabbing her arm. "We don't know what's out there. You crawl into this seat."

Sammy stared at him with a blank look for a moment before she shook her head. Dust winked at her right before he faded. He moved up through the roof, hovering just above it so he could look around. Below him, he could hear Sammy muttering under her breath and the car rock as she climbed over into the passenger seat.

Dust focused and settled back through the roof, this time into the driver's seat. He waited until he was sitting in the seat before he solidified again. Sammy released a startled squeak and glared at him.

"Next time, give me a little notice before you do that," she growled.

"Sorry," Dust replied with a crooked grin. "It looked okay outside, but I didn't take a really close look. Can you hand me a couple of cans of fruit before you go to sleep?"

Sammy glanced down at the half dozen empty cans and grimaced. He knew what she was thinking... that at the rate he was going through the fruit there wouldn't be anything left. She was probably right.

He reached out and took the cans from her. Within minutes, Sammy had pushed the seat back, pulled her jacket over her and was sound asleep. He opened one of the cans of fruit and drank the juice before devouring the contents. Once he was finished, he set the empty container on the dashboard and turned to stare at Sammy's relaxed face.

He could make out the sprinkling of freckles across her nose. She was pretty, he thought with a surprisingly warm feeling inside him. She was also smart and brave. Shoot, she had saved his life twice. He frowned when he thought about it, or rather about the devil dog. There had been something different about it.

Turning to look out the window, he stared off into the darkness. His gaze flickered back to Sammy before he glanced at Todd in the back seat. He would take a quick peek around outside to make sure everything was safe before he settled down for the night.

Fading again, he stepped out of the car before reforming. He didn't want to take the chance of waking Sammy and Todd, or anything else for that matter that might be out there. Glancing inside the car once more to reassure himself that Sammy and Todd were real, he turned and began walking toward the remains of the building.

He walked around it first, checking to make sure that nothing was hiding before he passed through the door. The floor was scattered with debris. Empty shelves lay twisted among broken bottles, empty wrappers, and pieces of the roof and walls.

Turning, he gazed around trying to see if there was anything worth salvaging. His eyes lit up when he spotted a scattering of maps along the floor near where the counter used to be. Climbing over a section of the roof, he scrambled over to where the circular wire display had stood.

He squatted down and picked up one of each one map. Standing up, he stuffed them into his back pocket. He spent the next twenty minutes walking through the inside. By the time he was done, he had picked up a bag full of stuff he thought they could use.

A soft sigh escaped him as he sunk his teeth into another Twinkie from the box he had found under a shelf. He paused at the door and frowned. He wondered if it was locked. Pushing against the door, he groaned until he saw that it said pull. Pulling, he was surprised when it opened.

Stepping out, he reached in and pulled another snack cake out of the box. Raising it to his teeth, he tore open the packaging and started eating it. He could feel the sugar high coursing through him. A surge of power swept through him as well now that he had eaten quite a bit.

He walked over to the shell of one of the trucks. Reaching into his pocket, he pulled out one of the napkins he had picked up. He wiped a small circle in the glass so he could peer inside.

A low curse escaped him and he fell backwards, tripping over his own feet as he jerked away. He ignored the contents of the bag as it spilled across the ground. Instead, his gaze remained locked on the pair of sightless eye sockets staring back at him.

"Oh, man," he muttered, standing back up and brushing off the back of his pants.

He swallowed. His gaze instinctively went to the car where Sammy and Todd were sleeping. He was glad that he had decided to explore tonight.

Releasing a deep breath, he quickly picked up all of the stuff he had collected. He placed the bag on the hood of the truck. He would need to check out all the vehicles. There was no way he wanted Sammy and Todd to see this.

A shuddered went through him when he tried to open the door. It was locked. Walking around to the other side, he tried the passenger side door. It was unlocked. Pulling it open, his face wrinkled in disgust.

Climbing in the truck, he shuddered again as he leaned across the skeletal remains and unlocked the door. He quickly pulled back and slid out of the truck. Dust walked back around to the driver's side door and opened it.

"Now, what?" He muttered, staring at the remains of the man. "I really don't want to touch this. I really, really don't."

He looked around, trying to decide what to do. His gaze paused on the store again. There had been several boxes of trash bags mixed in the mess. Turning, he jogged back to the store. Pulling on the door, he cursed when he hit the glass instead. He should have pushed. He shoved the door open and stepped over the debris until he found the section where he saw the boxes. He skipped the small bags and went straight to the huge lawn bags. The last thing he wanted was for the bag to get a hole in it.

"No dead guy's bones littering the ground," he said, picking up a second box just in case he needed it.

He looked down when he stepped on something. His eyes lit up with relief. It was only a plastic bag. He bent and picked the package up, curious when he saw something inside it. It was a pair of large, yellow rubber kitchen gloves.

He forgot to pull the door open - again. Pulling it open, he headed back to the truck. He quickly opened the package containing the gloves and pulled them on before he opened the box of garbage bags. Holding his breath, he pulled the thick, black bag over the head of the skeleton.

"This is so gross," Dust grumbled when part of the body pulled away.

It took him an hour to bag up the three bodies that he found in the remains of the vehicles. He decided he didn't have the time or the resources to bury the bodies. Instead, he carried them as far away from the store as he felt comfortable before dropping them. Not sure what he should do next, he stared at the six bags in uncertainty.

Releasing a sigh, he reached down and grabbed a handful of dirt. He tossed it on the bags before wiping his hand down his pant leg. His mouth opened and closed several times before he groaned.

"Rest in peace," he finally muttered before turning on his heel and jogging back to the store.

Dust grabbed the bag he had packed off the truck and walked back to the car. With a sigh, he realized he was either going to have to leave the bag outside of the car so he didn't make too much noise or take a chance of opening the car door and waking Todd and Sammy.

The problem was solved when Sammy suddenly opened the door and slid out of the car. Dust watched her stretch before she stepped away from the door. She stared suspiciously at the bag he was holding.

"I, uh... I decided to see if there was anything worth salvaging," he finally said.

"What did you find?" She asked softly.

Dust pulled out the box of Twinkies. "There's only two left," he replied with a crooked grin. "I was hungry."

Sammy stared at him for a moment before she shook her head and laughed. Reaching for one, she opened it and took a bite out of it before she released a sigh. Her hand reached for the second one before Dust could grab it.

"Thank you," she replied.

"You're welcome," Dust responded.

"For getting rid of the bodies, too," Sammy added as she walked toward the building.

"Oh," Dust replied, watching her as she walked toward the store. "Where are you going?"

Sammy glanced over her shoulder. "To the bathroom," she said.

Dust watched as Sammy walked away. He blinked when she pushed the door open and disappeared inside. He released a loud sigh and felt around in the sack for some potato chips. Opening the package of chips, he leaned back against the car and started eating while he waited for Sammy to return.

It's good not to be alone anymore, he thought.

Chapter 8

The storm:

Sammy leaned her head against the back seat and stared out the window. Dust was driving now and she had given up the front passenger seat to her little brother. He had been talking non-stop to Dust for the past couple of hours.

Her gaze briefly flickered to the front and she locked eyes with Dust in the mirror. A small smile twisted her lips when she saw the questioning look in his gaze. A moment later he broke contact to focus on the road in front of them.

"Sammy, can I have another snack cake?" Todd asked, glancing over the seat with a hopeful look.

"Just one more," Sammy murmured. "I don't want you getting sick to your stomach."

"I won't," Todd promised, turning back around to dig into the bag.

They had gone through the store one more time looking for things they could use while Dust had siphoned gas from the underground tanks. They had talked for a little while when she came back from using the bathroom. She was thankful that she had Todd for the past year. Dust had been all alone. She couldn't imagine not having someone else there to talk to. Sure, Todd was young, but he had given her a reason to keep going.

"What's that?" Todd asked, sitting up in the seat.

Sammy sat up and peered between the seats. A low curse escaped her when she saw the dark, rolling clouds and flashes of lightning. This wasn't your typical storm. It was a mega-storm. Since the comet, the weather had been extremely unpredictable. The nights changing from warm to freezing within minutes and the days were not much better.

"We need to find cover," Dust muttered under his breath. "Are there any towns nearby on the map?"

"I'll look," Sammy whispered, grabbing the map next to her and opening it up. Looking down, she ran her finger from the last town they went through and along the road in the direction they were traveling. They had to detour a few times because the main interstate was impassable in a few sections. Right now, they were on a back road. "I don't see anything," Sammy said with a frown.

"Look at that!" Todd exclaimed, pointing out the front window.

Sammy's head jerked up in time to see a line of lightning running in a long pattern along the ground. Swallowing, she watched the ground explode upward where it struck. She couldn't imagine any safe place from such a force.

"Dust," Sammy murmured, reaching out to touch his shoulder.

"I know," Dust muttered, turning left when another road came into sight.

"Where are you going?" Todd asked, looking out of his side of the window at the approaching storm.

"I'm going to see if I can find an overpass, bridge, or one of those huge culverts," Dust bit out through gritted teeth as the high winds began pushing on the car.

Sammy flinched when marble-size bits of ice hit the window next to her. She reached over and touched Todd's shoulder. She wanted him away from that side of the car in case the ice broke the window.

"Come back here and buckle up, Todd," she ordered, undoing his seatbelt.

"Okay," Todd replied in a slightly quivering voice.

Sammy helped Todd over the console between the seats and quickly buckled him up. Picking up the blanket that was on the floorboard, she opened it up and spread it over his lap. She winced when the hail grew stronger. She could hear it bouncing off the gas cans on the roof.

"Dust, we need to find shelter," she shouted above the growing storm.

"I know," Dust replied, jerking the wheel to the side to avoid some flying debris. "We can't stay out in this."

"Sammy!" Todd whimpered in terror when a bolt of lightning hit close to the road.

Sammy reached over and covered Todd's head as dirt and rocks pelted the front and side of the car. She felt Dust struggling to keep the car on the narrow, two-lane road. The tires kicked up dirt when the car ran off the road onto the soft shoulder. The car swerved back and forth for a moment as Dust tried not to flip the car. He had just straightened the car out when another explosion sounded behind them. Sammy twisted in time to see a portion of the road disintegrate behind them.

"Hang on," Dust yelled as he turned again, this time onto an old dirt road.

Sammy used one hand to hold onto the back of the seat and the other one she wrapped around Todd in an effort to keep from being thrown around despite the seatbelt she had on. Dust accelerated as more hail struck and lightning flashed. Sammy swore she could feel the back of the car start to lift up off the ground before Dust pulled away in a cloud of dirt.

She didn't know where he was going, she just hoped he found some place soon that would protect them from the elements. A cry escaped her when he fishtailed on a curve in the road and she felt her hold on Todd loosen. She was thrown sideways against the window. Pain exploded through her head when it hit with a sharp thump. Turning her head, she wished she had kept it straight when she saw the huge tornado bearing down on them.

"Dust," she whispered in horror.

"I know, Sammy," Dust replied in a grim tone. "I see it."

Sammy didn't say anything, she kept her eyes glued to the twister even as Dust turned the wheel again. This time, she held on to the seat in front of her with both hands. She was slowly counting, trying to measure the distance between them and the dark, swirling cloud.

"We're not going to make it," she whispered, her eyes growing bigger as the tornado expanded.

"Yes, we will," Dust replied, spying what he was looking for. "Hold on!"

At the corner of her eye, Sammy saw Todd reach out to grab the back of Dust's seat. A scream formed in her throat when she felt the car suddenly take a nose-dive. Forcing her eyes around to the front, she saw that Dust had left the road and was going down into a deep gully. Her eyes widened when she saw what he was aiming for, a huge culvert under the road. Overhead, large deposits of rocks, soil, and ice pounded on the car, leaving deep dents in the top. The front windshield suddenly cracked as several large chunks struck. Just as the sound of the tornado grew to a deafening roar, everything went black as the car skidded into the large, concrete cylinder beneath the road.

..*.

The dark shadows of the devil dogs emerged like ghostly shapes later that afternoon. Their sides moved rapidly in and out as they drew in panting breaths. The female had driven the remaining pack hard. She wanted to catch up with those she was hunting. One of the pack had fallen behind. She knew if she let it live the others would soon follow. She had killed and eaten it with a viciousness that warned the rest of the pack what their fate would be if they didn't keep up.

The Alpha paused as she smelled the approaching storm long before she saw it. Her pack could sense something, but they did not have the same awareness that she did. With a snarl, she drew to a halt outside of the dilapidated store. She had been following the faint scent of the metal beast that had carried the creatures off. With a snap of her jaws, her pack sought shelter in the remains of the building.

She would seek shelter, but not yet. Even with the growing wind, she could smell the one she sought, the one whose powers she wanted. Pressing her nose to the ground, she trotted back and forth until she found where he had gone. He had spent time at the other metal machines before moving off into the desert. Following the path of his scent, she soon came to the pile of black plastic bags.

Her gaze rose to the growing storm before returning to the bags. Stepping forward, she tore the first one open with her front claws. The remains of bone, dried flesh, and clothing pierced her senses. She reached forward and sank her teeth into the bone. Pulling it out, she quickly tore the material away from the remains and devoured the tough, dried out flesh.

A deep snarl escaped her when the growing wind sent a rain of sharp sand against her side. Her gaze returned to the growing storm. The hair on her nape rose at the electricity in the air. In the distance, bolts of lightning struck the ground. Realizing she wouldn't have time to finish feasting on the remains, she quickly dug a hole and buried the bags. She would eat afterwards.

She was just finishing when the first stinging blows of ice began to fall. Turning back toward her pack, she soon realized that she had misjudged the speed of the storm. Fighting against the wind, she noticed an outcropping of rocks. She focused, hating to use the limited amount of energy that she had, but knowing she had no choice. Dissolving, she breathed a sigh when the pain from the sharp ice and sand passed through her instead. Within minutes, she was cocooned inside a recess between the rocks. Reforming, she watched the storm with an appreciation for its intensity and power.

Power, she thought with a jerky, sudden awareness. *Yes, power. The… boy, he has power. Power that I want. The… others will give me the strength I need to defeat him. He… cares for them,* she realized with satisfaction. *That will be his weakness. He will not like it when I kill them.*

She scooted back further and closed her eyes against the stinging wind. She would rest. Her dissolving had taken more out of her than she realized. She had never dissolved for so long before. She would definitely need to feed after the storm.

I will eat, she thought as sleep pulled at her. *Then, I will hunt.*

Chapter 9

Not alone:

Dust rested his forehead on the steering wheel as the loud roar of the massive tornado moved closer. He could hear the rocks hitting the back windshield of the car. It was hard to breathe as it went over them. It felt like the twister was sucking all the air up out of the car. His head jerked up when he felt the car shift and begin to rise.

"Dust!" Todd cried in terror.

"I won't let anything happen to you or Sammy, Todd," Dust said in a hoarse voice, glancing over his shoulder.

He heard Sammy's soft gasp and knew his eyes must be glowing from the fear that flashed through them. He could feel the change in him. The power was surging through his system. Turning back around, he focused on his glowing hands.

The car shifted in the air for a moment before it settled back down. He could feel the heat radiating out from him. His teeth gritted as he battled for control of the energy spreading like a fiery wave outward. He watched as if in slow motion as a soft blue light stretched outward to form a partial dome over the car. Sweat beaded on his brow as he fought to maintain it. The sound of the wind and the rain of debris hitting the car faded as it struck the shield instead.

"Sammy," Todd whispered in awe.

"Shush," Sammy replied under her breath.

Dust looked in the rearview mirror at Sammy. He could see the fear, but he could also see that she knew that he was doing what he had promised – he was protecting her and Todd. That knowledge gave him the strength to push away the darkness clouding the edge of his vision.

It seemed like hours later, but was really just minutes, before the faint sound of the storm moving away echoed through the culvert. Dust's body shook from the force of expending so much energy. His knuckles were as blue as the field of energy where he had them wrapped around the black plastic steering wheel.

"It's gone," Sammy whispered, tentatively reaching out to touch his shoulder. "You can stop now."

"I…," Dust started to say before he just nodded.

The moment he released the power, his body slumped like a limp noodle. He was as weak as a newborn kitten. This was far worse than back in town.

"Dust?" Sammy asked when his head fell sideways against the driver's door.

"F… food," Dust muttered, closing his eyes as nausea welled up inside him.

Realizing he wasn't going to be able to keep it at bay, he struggled to open the door with a trembling hand. He fumbled for the release on the seat belt that was holding him in the seat as the door swung open. It snapped free and he rolled out of the car, hitting the ground hard as his body starting heaving in waves. There was nothing to eject. He had used up all of the food he had eaten plus some. The force of the dry heaves sent his body into spasms.

"Dust!" Sammy cried out as she scrambled out of the car and ran around to kneel down next to him. "Oh, Dust."

"Food," he wheezed, trying to pull in enough air to talk.

"Todd, get a soda," Sammy called out in a panic.

"Here you go, Sammy," Todd whispered, handing his sister a can of soda through the opened driver's door.

"Drink this," Sammy ordered.

Dust heard the click of the metal tab on the can and the fizz of the sugary drink a second before Sammy held it to his lips. He panted heavily several times before he felt he could take a sip without throwing it back up. The moment the liquid hit his taste buds, he felt an almost savage hunger sweep through him. He pushed up off the ground onto his knees and greedily grabbed for the can, spilling some of the contents on his shirt.

"Slow down," Sammy whispered in a soothing voice. "That's it. Let me help you."

Dust forced his hands down to his lap, clenching them, and let Sammy hold the can while he drank as fast as he could. He finished the can in seconds. She must have realized that he needed more because she ordered Todd to get her another one before he finished the first. Three cans later, he was able to sit on the ground next to the car with his back against the open driver's side.

"Here you go, Dust," Todd said, holding out several bags of chips.

Dust looked up at Todd and gave him a weak smile. "Thanks, Todd," he whispered in a rough voice.

"No problem," Todd replied, hanging out of the back seat window. "That was even cooler than the disappearing through the door thing that you do."

Dust gave a dry laugh as he shakily opened a bag of potato chips. He reached in and grabbed a handful before stuffing the lot of them in his mouth. A soft moan of pleasure escaped him as the salty chips sent a flood of energy into his system.

"That good, huh?" Sammy teased, sitting down across from him.

"Yeah," Dust mumbled around the mouthful of crunchy snack food.

"I smell gas," Todd complained.

Sammy lifted her head and sniffed the air. A frown creased her brow and she stood up. Dust groaned and pushed off the ground with one hand while hanging onto the bag of chips with the other. He could smell it now, too.

"It looks like one of the cans was punctured," Sammy said, standing on the edge of the driver's door.

"We need to put it in the gas tank before it runs out," Dust muttered, tilting the bag to refill his mouth.

"I can do it," Sammy said, glancing over her shoulder at him with a chuckle. "You finish eating."

"Okay," Dust agreed with a salty grin before turning to look at Todd. "Do we have any more cans of fruit?"

Todd nodded. "Yeah, we have some pears and some apricots," he said, sliding back down to look inside one of the bags in the very back of the car. "How many do you want?"

"Five," Dust automatically replied before he glanced up at Sammy when she turned from releasing the leaking gas can to stare at him with a raised eyebrow. "Two," he hastily corrected. "I'll take two."

He stepped back when Sammy stepped down from the door frame with the gas can. She tilted it to keep the dime-size holes in the top of the plastic container from pouring down over her. He quickly stepped around her to open the gas cap before moving back against the side of the culvert again.

He watched as she extended the spout and slowly tilted it so that the gas went into the tank and not all over the ground. Popping open the first can of fruit, he drank the heavy syrup before picking out the tasty tidbits. With each mouthful, he was feeling better.

"Thank you again," Sammy said.

Dust paused and frowned. Her head was tilted slightly away from him so he couldn't see her face. He licked his lips and swallowed the fruit in his mouth before he spoke.

"For what?" He asked in confusion.

Sammy glanced over her shoulder at him for a second before refocusing on what she was doing. He saw her draw in a deep breath. She was silent for a second before he heard her softly spoken words.

"For saving us again," she replied.

Dust set the empty fruit can down on the ground by his feet and took a step closer to Sammy. He gently reached out and took the nearly empty container from her hands and set it down on the ground next to the tire. Turning her around to face him, he lifted his hand to gently tilt her head back so that she was forced to look at him.

"You never have to thank me for that," Dust whispered, looking down at her.

Dust wasn't consciously aware that his hand was sliding along Sammy's jaw and around to the back of her neck. Or that he was pulling her towards him. All he was aware of was that he was slowly drowning in her hazel eyes. Her eyes widened and her lips parted when he started to bend his head. Deep down, he knew he should stop, but that thought seemed to evaporate as fast as it formed in his mind.

Her eyes fluttered for a brief second before they closed as his lips settled over hers in a kiss that shocked them both. He had never kissed a girl before, and if he had to guess, Sammy had never been kissed either. He wasn't real sure what to do, just that he liked the feel of her in his arms as they wrapped around her and the soft touch of her lips against his. He would have taken more time to explore if he hadn't felt a tug on his left arm.

Pulling back, he looked to the side with a dazed expression. Todd was staring back at him with an expression that was a mixture of distaste and amusement.

"Why are you kissing Sammy?" Todd asked, tilting his head and staring up at Dust.

Dust turned to look down at Sammy. She was looking away from her little brother and had bowed her head so he couldn't see her face again. His hand rose and he ran his fingers down along her cheek.

"Because I wanted to," Dust murmured.

Sammy's head jerked up and she stared at him in silence. A look of uncertainty and worry darkened her eyes. He wished he could wave his hand and erase it. He was about to say something to her when a sense of warning swept through him. Turning, he pushed Sammy protectively between him and the car. He turned his body and held his hands up, palms facing outward to show he was unarmed, as several dark shapes appeared on both sides of the culvert.

"I told you I saw a car coming down the road," a deep voice said from the front of the car.

Chapter 10

Uncertainty:

Dust stared uneasily as four men stepped into the large culvert. He kept Sammy behind him. Todd must have realized that this could also be dangerous as he had disappeared back into the car and was crouched down in the seat. Glancing back and forth, Dust waited to see which one spoke first.

"That was some fancy driving for a boy," an older man reflected.

Dust noticed that he stopped about four feet away, keeping a safe space between them. The man looked to be in his early fifties. He was partially bald on top and had a weathered face like he had spent most of his life outside in the sun. He was dressed in a pair of faded jeans with a dark red button up shirt and a pair of well-worn boots. There was nothing unusual about the man's clothing. What caught and held Dust's attention was the rifle in the man's hand.

"Thank you," Dust murmured, shifting to the left a little when another man tried to get a good look at Sammy.

"Where you from?" The man asked.

"South," Dust replied.

A soft chuckle from another one of the men drew Dust's attention. He stiffened when the younger man pointed his gun at him. Instinctively, his hands clenched in preparation.

"He doesn't talk much, does he, Beau?" The young man chuckled.

"Shut up, Alex, and keep your damn gun pointed down," Beau replied in a curt tone. "How many times do I have to tell you that? You're going to shoot somebody one of these days."

"What's the girl's name?" Another one of the men asked, trying to get a better look at Sammy.

Dust turned to look at the man with a piercing stare. "Why do you want to know?" He asked.

"Back off, Howard," Beau said with a wave of his hand. "If you haven't figured it out, my name is Beau. I'm in charge of the compound. That is Alex, Howard, and Randolph."

Dust turned to look at each man as Beau pointed to them. He nodded his head to each man, but didn't say anything. These were the first people other than Sammy and Todd that they'd met. They appeared normal, but then again, so did he. At least, he thought he did. It took a minute for him to realize that Beau was waiting for him to respond in kind. Wiping his right hand down his pant leg, he drew in a deep breath before he spoke.

"I'm Dust," he said in a husky voice. "This is Sammy. Todd's in the car."

Dust watched as Beau nodded and glanced in the car at Todd. Todd murmured a quiet greeting when Dust said his name. His lips tightened when the man looked appraisingly at Sammy before he looked through the back window of the car at the items they had gathered.

"We might as well get back to the compound," Beau commented. "We got caught out in the storm as well. Randolph and I will ride with you while Alex and Howard drive the trucks."

"Aw, Beau," Alex grumbled, shooting Sammy a grin. "I wanted to sit with the girl."

Beau pursed his lips. "That's why you are driving the other truck."

"No," Dust said in a husky, but determined voice. "We'll follow you, but no one rides with us."

"Like hell…," Alex started to say, but stopped when Beau chuckled.

"No, the boy's smart. He knows to be cautious. I wish I could say that about some of the others," Beau commented.

"Others?" Sammy asked, speaking for the first time. "How many others?"

Beau smiled at Sammy. "Ten," he replied.

"Ten," Sammy repeated her eyes widening at the thought of there being so many others in one place.

Dust reached back and touched Sammy's arm. It was just enough for her to know that he wanted her to get in the car. Sammy understood his silent message and slid along the car so that she could crawl through the driver's side to the passenger's side. Only when she was safely in the seat did Dust step up to the door.

"We'll follow you," he told Beau with a nod of his head.

"Let's go, boys," Beau said, jerking his head to the others. "Just drive forward. This ditch goes along for about a half mile before there's a cutoff where you can drive out."

Dust nodded and started the car, inching it forward behind the men. He blinked in the bright sunlight. Ahead of him, he could see another large culvert where the other section of road crossed over. It was hard to see what the land above looked like after the tornado. It took a little while for the men to turn the trucks they were driving around. They must have seen the storm coming and headed for the gulch as well, only from the opposite direction.

"Do you think it is safe?" Sammy asked, staring at the two trucks.

"I don't know," Dust admitted reluctantly.

"I don't like this, Sammy," Todd said, leaning forward. "You couldn't see the other guy, but he kept staring at you."

"He wasn't the only one," Dust muttered under his breath.

Sammy giggled and reached over to lay her hand on his thigh. An intense wave of possessiveness swept through Dust at her touch. She and Todd were his to protect. Sammy may not have seen Randolph's intense look, but Dust had. A part of him wanted to take off, just keep heading north, while another part of him wondered if he was just being paranoid.

"Thank you, both of you, for looking out for me," Sammy replied in a quiet voice. "Why don't we see what it is like? If we don't like it, we take off and keep heading north."

"I think we should do that now," Todd said in a sullen voice before he sat back in his seat.

Dust looked in the rearview mirror at Todd. The little boy sat with his arms crossed and a mutinous, stubborn pout on his face. He winked at Todd to let him know that he felt the same way. Still, if Sammy wanted to give it a couple of days, it might be worth it. They could all use some decent sleep and a hot meal.

"Todd, hide the food we've found under the other stuff," Dust ordered as another worry struck him.

"Why?" Todd asked, already undoing his seatbelt so he could start moving things around.

"You're afraid they'll take our food?" Sammy asked, biting her bottom lip and turning to watch Todd.

Dust nodded. "We just need to be careful. If they take our food, who knows when we'll find any more," he said, glancing at her. "I want you and Todd to stay close to me. We can't let them separate us."

Sammy nodded. "Okay," she whispered, glancing back out the front window as they began to slow down.

None of them said anything else as they drew to a stop along a flat area with the remains of several buildings. The truck in the front paused in front of a long half domed building. It looked like it had been half buried on each side except the front.

“What is it?” Sammy asked, leaning forward and bracing her hands on the dash.

Dust shook his head. “I’m not sure,” he muttered, bending forward as well so he could see better. “Just, stay close to me.”

“We will,” Sammy promised, sitting back and resting her hand on his leg again.

Dust swallowed when he saw one of the men open the double doors. He eased his foot off the brake and let the car roll forward behind the other two as they entered the building. There was something about Sammy’s touch that calmed him while at the same time confused him.

He thought about the kiss he had given her earlier. He didn’t know why he had kissed her. Heck, he didn’t even realize what he was doing until his lips touched hers. It had been… amazing! He was startled when he felt a warmth deep inside him and his… Dust glanced down at his lap in shock.

“Dust, stop!” Sammy said, moving her hand to brace against the dash again.

Dust’s head jerked up, and he slammed his foot on the brake just inches from the truck in front of him. He felt his cheeks warm and was thankful for the dark interior of the building so that Sammy couldn’t see him blushing. Shifting uncomfortably in his seat, he hoped that the rest of his body returned to normal before it was light enough to see.

“I don’t see no one else,” Todd said, breaking into his thoughts.

Dust looked around the interior of the building. Dozens of large crates were stacked along the walls. Further down, he could see two more trucks parked. They were larger box trucks used for moving and hauling stuff. He reached for the door handle and pushed it opened. Twisting, he breathed a sigh of relief when he felt his body return to normal.

He grabbed the back door when Todd pushed it open and slid out. Closing it, Dust glanced over at Sammy as she got out of the passenger side and closed the door. Reaching down, he pulled the keys out of the ignition and pocketed them before pressing the lock button on the door and closing it.

"This way," Beau said, nodding his head. "The rest of you unload the trucks and bring the items downstairs."

"Downstairs?" Sammy whispered, reaching out her hand to grab a hold of Todd's cold fingers.

Dust blinked. Now, he remembered where he had seen a building like this. It had been in one of his games. He reached out and stopped Sammy when she started to walk ahead of him.

"It's an old military silo," he whispered, nodding to the end of the building. They had buildings like this. They must have moved this one in front of the entrance to the silo."

Fear swept across Sammy's face and she pulled back, dragging Todd with her. Dust could feel her trembling and she was shaking her head. He slid his hand down her arm and grasped her free hand.

"I'll be with you," he promised, squeezing her fingers. "I told you I'd protect you and Todd."

Sammy visibly swallowed and nodded her head. "I know, but aren't they really deep? This isn't like the storm shelter behind the house. This goes way down in the ground, doesn't it?" She asked in a barely audible voice.

"Come on, Dust," Beau called out. "I'll introduce the three of you to the others."

"Yeah, it does," Dust responded before he started forward. "Together."

"Together," Sammy and Todd murmured at the same time as they stepped up to the narrow staircase leading down into the ground.

Chapter 11

Downward:

Dust kept his eyes on the man in front of him. He didn't like that Alex and Howard had stayed back in the upper area, but he liked it even less that Randolph was walking behind them. There was something about the guy that rubbed Dust the wrong way. It was more than the way he looked at Sammy. There was just a feeling about the guy that made the hair on the back of his neck stand up.

"Are you okay?" Sammy whispered, leaning down over his shoulder on the steps.

Dust squeezed Sammy's hand and nodded. He didn't want to talk in the narrow stairwell. They went down several flights before they reached an open doorway. He paused for a moment, taking in the large, circular room. It looked like a command center of some type.

"This way," Beau said, glancing over his shoulder. "We still have a long way to go. This room is just used for getting ready to go topside."

Dust nodded. He heard Todd whisper to Sammy in excitement. He also felt the tremble in Sammy's hand as they moved deeper underground. She was squeezing his fingers to the point they were beginning to grow numb.

"I was stationed here back in the early sixties. After the Cold War ended the government sold these off. I figured it was a good deal, especially since they were selling them real cheap. I've been working on remodeling it for the past twenty years. After fragments of the comet hit the Earth, I realized it was the best investment I had ever made," Beau said, walking down a wide corridor to a thick, red metal door.

"Why didn't the government warn everybody about the comet ahead of time?" Sammy asked in a husky voice.

Beau turned as he reached the end of the corridor and gazed down at Sammy. A bitter smile curved his lips. Dust watched as Beau pulled on a cord that ran through the wall and paused before he pulled it again.

"What good would it have done?" Beau asked in a soft voice. "All the governments of the world thought the world was about to end. They were too busy trying to save their own asses to give a damn about ours. Besides, it wouldn't have done anything but cause mass chaos. What is more humane? Telling people that they are going to die or letting them continue on with their daily lives, oblivious to what tomorrow will bring?"

"But, we didn't all die?" Todd murmured, staring up at Beau. "We're alive."

"Yeah, we are," Beau replied with a smile. "But there are a lot fewer of us than there used to be."

"Some are different, too," Randolph muttered behind them.

"That's enough, Rand," Beau snapped, turning when the door opened. "Two rings, pause, two rings and someone will open the door."

Dust nodded, glancing over his shoulder at Rand before he started after Beau. A frown creased his brow as he tried to decipher what Rand was talking about. Did he know about other people like him? If he did, neither he nor Beau looked too happy about it.

The next hour was spent moving from section to section of the old silo. Dust made a mental note in case they needed to find a way out. Unfortunately, it looked like there were only two ways; through the seventy ton doors covering the launch bay or through the door they came through.

"You'll each be given chores to do," Beau said as he finally stopped along one section near the bottom. "This floor and the one below it are for sleeping. We've put up walls between to give people a bit of privacy. The men sleep here and the women and kids on the section below."

"Women? Kids? There are more here?" Sammy asked in surprise.

Beau nodded. "Yes, there's two women and three kids; two boys and a girl," he explained.

Dust frowned and looked around. "I thought you said there were ten people here," he said. "That makes nine, counting you, Howard, Alex, and Randolph."

Beau's mouth tightened into a flat, hard line. "The other one isn't any concern of yours. Just stay out of the last area. It is off limits. I've got to make sure that Howard and Alex get everything out of the trucks. The cover we've built does a good job of protecting them, but the storms can be unpredictable. I want to get as many supplies as we can down below," he replied. "You can spend today getting familiar with the silo. I'll have jobs assigned to you starting tomorrow. I'll send one of the women around to show you to your room, Sammy. Todd, you can stay with Dust."

Dust moved so that he was standing in front of Sammy. "Sammy should stay with me as well," he said, staring back at Beau with a frown.

Beau returned his gaze, not saying anything for a moment before he shook his head. "I'm sorry, son, Sammy will have to stay with the other women. It's the law," he said with a slight edge to his tone that told Dust he wouldn't change his mind.

"Whose law?" Dust asked, clenching his right hand by his side.

Beau's eyes narrowed on Dust's face. "Mine," he finally said. "You don't follow the laws, you are out of here."

Dust didn't respond. He could tell the man standing in front of him was serious. Yet, there was a quiet warning in his tone as well.

"Rand will show you where you can get some clothes and bedding and give you a run down on how we do things," Beau stated, turning away.

Dust watched as Beau disappeared back the way they came. He glanced around the large circular room. It was partitioned into sections with the center set up as a common seating area while the outer parts were sectioned off into rooms.

"You and the boy can use that one," Rand said stiffly. "It is a little bigger and we can fit another cot into it. Once he gets used to things, he can move into his own room. Alex is on your right and Howard is on the left. I'm next, followed by Beau's room here on the end."

Dust nodded, glancing at the second door across the room. It was about as far from the entrance as they could put him. He turned when Rand started to walk by him.

"I'll show you where the supplies are again," Rand said. "Then, I've got work to do. Dinner is in two hours."

"Dust has to…," Todd started to say before he clamped his mouth closed when Dust sharply shook his head in warning.

Rand's eyes narrowed suspiciously on Dust before he turned that same sharp, intense look on Todd. Dust bit his lip. Something warned him that he shouldn't say anything about needing to frequently eat.

"Dust has to… what?" Rand asked Todd, turning until he stood facing the boy.

Todd swallowed and looked nervously at Dust. Clenching his hand at his side again, Dust thought about what he could do if the situation became dangerous. If he needed to, he could knock Rand out, grab Todd and Sammy and head back up through the silo. He started when he felt Sammy's hand on his lower back. For a minute, he had forgotten she was there. She had become very quiet after Beau explained she wouldn't be allowed to stay with him and her brother.

"Dust has to make sure he stays away from peanuts," Sammy interjected. "He has an allergy to them."

"Yeah, he's allergic to peanuts," Todd agreed with a nervous grin. "Isn't that right, Dust?"

Dust relaxed and nodded. "I break out," he said.

Rand stared back and forth between the three of them before he shrugged his shoulders and turned away again. Dust relaxed his fingers when Sammy slid her hand into his. He'd have to remember not to eat anything with peanuts in it even though he loved peanut butter. With a sigh, he started forward.

"As soon as we can, I want to get out of here," Sammy whispered in his ear. "This place doesn't feel right."

A relieved smile curved Dust's lips and he gave a brief nod. Sammy released his hand when a woman stepped into the room and gave her a nervous smile. It took everything inside Dust not to protest when the woman who said her name was Maria led Sammy away.

His gaze followed her until Rand started to explain what he was allowed to get out of the supply room. Nodding, Dust decided that tonight, he was going to have to do a little exploring after the others were asleep. He'd start with the very bottom floor.

Chapter 12

A Dark Foe:

Dust lay in the dark listening to Todd's soft snores. They had eaten with the rest of the group before retiring to their room. Sammy had been quiet, but she gave him a small nod to let him know that she was alright. She had also given him a roughly drawn map to the lower section where she was staying.

Rolling onto his side, he pulled the penlight out of his pocket and flicked it on. She was almost directly below him. He turned the light off and put the penlight back in his pocket before he focused. He felt the odd tingle in his body just before he faded.

Rising from the bed, he glanced down at Todd's peaceful form once more before he passed through the thin door of their room. He continued across the open common area until he reached the outer section. Turning right, he quickly made his way down the stairwell to the lower section where Sammy and the other women and children stayed.

Pulling the image of the map up in his head, he walked over to the third door from the entrance. He paused to look around. Stella, one of the other women that he had met earlier, was sitting by a small lamp. She was patching clothing. Dust froze when she paused and looked around with a frown before she returned her attention to the shirt she was working on.

He passed through the door to Sammy's room and scanned it to make sure she was alone before he solidified. A grin curved his lips when Sammy covered her mouth to smother the squeak when he suddenly appeared. She scowled at him before she waved him closer.

"Here," she whispered, holding out several candy bars. "I had these in my bag. I couldn't take anything from the supply room. Maria and Stella count everything."

"I'll get more from the car later," Dust whispered with a smile of thanks as he ripped one of the chocolate bars open and devoured it. "They don't feed us much, that's for sure."

"I noticed that," Sammy replied with a grim look. "How is Todd?"

"He's asleep," Dust assured her. "I'm going to go take a look around. I'll be back in a couple of hours."

Sammy nodded and scooted back on the bed. She drew her knees up to her chin and stared at him. He could see that she was scared, but she was trying to hide it.

"Where are you going?" She asked in a husky voice.

Dust reached out and touched her cheek with his fingers. "Just to look around," he whispered. "It will be alright. We'll leave tomorrow if you want."

Sammy nodded and leaned her cheek into his hand. "I'm scared, Dust. What if they don't let us go? What if they try to stop us?" She asked.

"They won't," Dust assured her. "Beau said we could leave if we wanted."

Sammy swallowed and nodded. "Just… be careful," she said.

"I will. I promise," he replied, standing up and winking at her before he focused and faded from sight.

He passed through the door again. This time, the room was empty. The shirt that Stella had been working on was lying neatly folded on top of a basket of other clothing. He walked out of the circular room and turned toward the stairwell leading down to the last level. Swallowing, he glanced over his shoulder before he started down the steps.

..*

Thirty miles away, ten dark shadows paused. The one in the front stepped forward onto the rise and stared down along the narrow, two-lane road. She could feel the other creature, the one she hunted. It was a faint pull, but she could feel him calling to her.

Turning, she snarled at one of the other devil dogs. It was her beta. It would support her to the death.

Storm.

It's thoughts washed through her mind like a fuzzy picture, but she knew what it was saying. Her gaze turned back to the massive storm that was churning in the distance. It was slowly moving away, but it was still too dangerous for them to approach. Without cover, her pack would be defenseless.

Search, she ordered.

Her Beta turned and growled to several of the black shapes lying behind her before taking off at a run. She watched as they disappeared over the rise and down along the road. Hunger pulled at her.

There had not been much to eat at the rubble of the buildings they had left miles behind. She had finished eating the flesh that had been in the bags, but it had not been enough to build her strength. The storm and the necessity for them to hunt had also slowed down her ability to track the vehicle. The second storm in the distance was worse than the first one. This one was more dangerous, but it would also force the ones she hunted to seek shelter as well. She could feel it.

A low whine from one of the dogs behind her drew her attention. It was hungry. Her eyes blazed as they ran over the beast. Turning, she trotted back to where it was lying. The dog immediately dropped its head down and tucked its tail between its legs before offering its throat in submission.

A primitive urge swept through her and she wanted to rip into the vulnerable tissue. It was the new, cognizant part of her that cautioned her to wait. She would need numbers when she confronted the two-legged creatures again. Once they were eliminated, she could kill this one. Until then, she would have to wait.

A low snarl of disapproval filled the air before she focused on the cringing beast. A low yelp escaped it, but it didn't move as she bent closer. Her mouth watered at the thought of burying it into the soft flesh. She almost ignored her need for numbers verses her need for sustenance. Her mouth opened to reveal razor-sharp teeth. Her head started downward before it jerked up at the faint sound of her Beta's howl. It had found the trail.

***

Dust paused outside of another massive red door. He frowned as he stared at it. Solidifying, he placed a hand against it and thought for a moment. He was about to open it when he heard the faint sound of footsteps and a flicker of light coming down the stairs.

Stepping back, he faded again and waited. A minute later, Beau and Alex came into view. He was carrying a small tray in one hand and a flashlight in the other. Alex was carrying a shotgun.

"I don't know why we don't just kill it," Alex grumbled. "It's just eating food that could be for the rest of us."

"Shut up, Alex," Beau growled. "Open the door."

"What if it got loose again?" Alex asked, setting his shotgun down next to the door.

"Then, you can kill it," Beau replied in exasperation. "I warned it that if it tried to escape again, that there wouldn't be a second chance."

"The only reason you haven't is because…," Alex started to say before he snapped his mouth shut. "Sorry, Beau."

"Just shut up, Alex, and stay focused," Beau ordered, again. "I'll go in, you stay by the door like you normally do. If it tries to get out, close the door and seal it."

"I know. I know," Alex grumbled, grabbing his gun and pulling the door open.

Dust curiously listened as the two talked back and forth with each other. He moved silently past Alex and followed Beau into the area. This one was different from the others. It had been left unfinished. Cold, gray concrete covered the walls, floor, and ceiling. In the center was a thick support column. Wrapped around it was a heavy chain. The entire room was illuminated by three bright shop lights mounted to the ceiling.

Dust slid back along the wall just inside the door and waited. He watched as Beau cautiously stepped into the room and looked around. A movement out of the corner of his eye drew his attention back to the solid beam in the center of the room.

"Josie, I've brought you some food," Beau called out, setting the tray down on the ground and sliding it toward the beam.

A slender hand slid along the concrete post before a tangle of red hair appeared. Dust drew in a swift breath of air when a pair of vivid green eyes stared back at Beau. The body of a young girl, slightly older than him and Sammy, stepped out from around the pillar. Her eyes narrowed on where Alex stood at the door with his shotgun aimed at her.

"I thought you forgot about me," she whispered in a husky voice.

Dust frowned when he saw the thick chains around both of her wrists. His hands curled at the sight of the thin body. He wondered what she had done to deserve being chained like an animal.

"Just eat, girl, so I can take the tray back," Beau ordered.

Josie slowly sank to her knees and picked up the food. It didn't take her long to devour the meager offering. She stood up and kicked the tray across the floor, ignoring Alex when he stepped forward in warning. A menacing smile curved her lips as she tilted her head and looked over Beau's shoulder.

"What's the matter, Alex? Feeling a little hot under the collar?" Josie asked with a soft laugh. "I can make you hotter if you like."

"Josie," Beau growled in warning.

Josie's gaze swept along the wall where Dust was standing. He saw her frown for a second before her gaze locked on Beau's face. The tension in the air grew the longer they stared at each other.

"Go away," she finally muttered, looking away. "You don't give me enough food to fight."

"If I did, you'd kill us all," Beau retorted in a soft tone.

Josie gave him a malicious grin before she stepped back to the center pillar where the chains were attached. She ran her hand along it, pausing before she disappeared again. Dust watched as Beau bent and picked up the tray before he started to turn back toward the door.

"Wouldn't you?" Josie's whispered question resonated through the room.

Beau paused and turned back to her. Dust waited, starting to feel the drain from being in his current form pulling on him. He clenched his fist, focusing to keep the form.

"Wouldn't I what?" Beau asked in a harsh voice.

Josie glanced over her shoulder and stared at Beau. "Wouldn't you kill all of us if we starved you and treated you like some unnatural beast? Wouldn't you, dad?"

Beau's face stiffened and he turned on his heel. Dust released a deep breath when the door closed behind them. He rested his head against the wall and closed his eyes, debating if he should solidify and eat a candy bar now, or after he got out of the room.

"Don't let them know what you are," Josie's voice echoed in the room. "They won't chain you up. They'll kill you, like they did the others."

Dust was so shocked when Josie reappeared around the pillar that he lost his hold on his form and reappeared. He stared at Josie. With shaky fingers, he reached into his pocket and pulled out the other two candy bars that Sammy had given him. Tearing one open, he quickly ate it. He started to unwrap the other one, but something stopped him. Glancing up, he saw Josie's gaze locked on the precious energy in his hand.

He took a step forward, pausing for a moment before he pushed his reservations away. He wanted, needed, answers. Why was she chained up down here? What did she mean when she said they had killed the others? Was she like him? And most important, was Beau really her father?

"I'm Dust," he said, holding out the candy bar as he came to a stop in front of her.

She hesitated a moment before she reached out and took the chocolate out of his hand. Ripping it open, she quickly devoured the sweet treat. He watched as she licked her fingers even as she kept her gaze on him.

"I'm Josie," she finally responded. "How long have you been here?"

"We just arrived this afternoon," he admitted, frowning at the chains hanging from her arms. "Why do they keep you chained up?"

Josie tilted her head and smiled at Dust. "Because they are afraid of me," she replied with a bitter laugh.

"Should they be?" He asked curiously.

Dust studied Josie's face for a moment before he looked around the pillar. Stepping to the side, he saw an old mattress on the ground and some blankets. There were some other small items, a bowl of water, a towel, some additional clothing, but not much else. His gaze swept the back wall. A makeshift toilet was up against the wall. He started to turn back to look at

Josie when he caught a line of dark streaks along the other side of the wall and ceiling. They looked like burn marks.

"Not at first, but they should be terrified now," she retorted as she followed his gaze.

"Fire?" He murmured in a puzzled voice.

"I shouldn't have wasted my energy," Josie replied with a shrug.

Dust turned to look at Josie again as he pieced together what she was saying without really telling him. His gut feeling that this wasn't a good place to be was growing. Now, it looked like they would have someone else tagging along with them. There was no way he could leave Josie imprisoned here, especially if her only offense was being different like him.

"You said there were others. Were they like you… and me?" Dust asked.

Josie gave Dust a grim, sad smile and wearily sank down onto the mattress. She pulled the chain up next to her and leaned her head back against the concrete beam. He stepped closer and squatted down so he could see her face. She blinked several times before she closed her eyes.

"Yes," she said in a husky voice. "There were five of us. We didn't know what had happened. Dad… Beau… killed Ethan first. He said it was the work of the devil and that we'd turn into beasts, like some of the animals we saw in the first weeks after the impact. Tim, Karen, and Mr. Beckman were the next three they hunted down." She opened her eyes and looked at Dust. "He wanted to kill me, but he couldn't. I'm his flesh and blood. But even that won't save me if I try to leave again. He'll hunt me down and kill me just like he did the others."

"How can he tell?" Dust asked, staring back at the dark marks.

"If you are like us, you need more food than normal. He'll watch you. That's one reason they count everything. They don't eat much either," she whispered, groaning and falling to the side on the bed. "I'm always so hungry."

Dust watched as she curled up into a ball. Her arms were protectively wrapped around her waist. Making a decision, he rose to his feet.

"Listen, my friends and I are getting out of here. You can come with us," he said, looking down at Josie as she rolled onto her back.

"I can't dissolve like you," she whispered. "I'm too weak to do anything."

"I'll get you some food," Dust promised. "We have some in our car. I'll bring it down to you. But, you've got to promise not to do anything until we are ready to go. I won't endanger Sammy and Todd."

Josie slowly sat up and pushed her hair back from her face. He could see the hope and fear in her eyes. She bit her lip before she nodded.

"Are they like us? What can they do?" She asked in a husky voice.

Dust shook his head. "They aren't like us, but I swore I'd protect them. Sammy saved my life. I won't do anything that will put her or her little brother in danger," he informed her with a look of warning.

Josie finally nodded. "You get me out of here, and I'll help you," she promised in a soft voice.

"I'll be back," Dust whispered, stepping back and fading. "I promise."

He was almost to the outer wall when he heard Josie call out his name. He turned, but didn't reform. He knew she could sense him.

"You'd better come back, Dust," Josie whispered. "Please… Don't leave me here to die."

Dust swallowed and turned away. He had a lot more exploring to do before the night was out and still needed to get up to the car for some food before returning to Sammy to let her know what he found out. Passing through the wall, Dust felt a growing sense of urgency. There was something else out there. He could feel it. Even tucked deep in the ground, he could feel the threat getting closer.

Hunted, he thought as he moved up the stairwell. *I feel like I'm being hunted.*

Chapter 13

A Strange Feeling:

It didn't take Dust long to check out each level. There were times when he reformed to conserve his energy. He found the room where the weapons were stored. A grin curved his lips when he saw the array of bows mounted on the wall and the various types of arrows. Sammy would be in heaven if she could get her hands on half of the supply.

After that, he moved to the food storage area. It was packed with all types of canned and packaged items. He didn't spend long in that room. It was too tempting to grab some of the food and eat it. Instead, he worked his way up to the first door. He faded through it and continued up the stairs.

He paused when he saw a light in the front section and heard some voices. It was Randolph and Howard. Wishing he still had one of the candy bars that Sammy had given him for an extra kick, he faded and moved closer.

"What do you think of the new kids?" Howard asked.

Dust watched as Howard placed a card down on the table. Randolph didn't say anything at first. His gaze swept around the small room, pausing on the guns propped up next to each man. Randolph picked up the card Howard had discarded before he responded.

"The younger boy doesn't bother me none, it's the older one I don't trust. There is something about him," Randolph muttered.

"What about the girl? She's kind of pretty, don't you think?" Howard asked with a grin. "It's nice to have a young one here; well, besides you-know-who."

"I want the girl. She's going to be mine. I already told Beau I was claiming her," Randolph stated in a blunt tone.

Howard groaned and shook his head. "You can't just call dibs on her. That's not fair to the rest of us," he complained with a frown.

"Well, I am," Randolph replied, setting down several cards. "Straight flush."

Howard grimaced and looked down at his cards. Dust moved to the other side of the doorway when Randolph frowned and glanced his way. A sense of panic swept through him when Randolph laid his cards down on the table and reached for the rifle next to him. Had he partially reformed and Randolph caught a glimpse of him as he moved across the doorway?

"What is it?" Howard asked, looking up at Randolph with a scowl. "You feeling weird things again, Rand?"

"Shut up, Howard," Randolph growled, shooting a nasty look at the other man. "I thought I saw something."

"There ain't nothing there," Howard grumbled. "Beau doesn't come to relieve us for at least another four hours and the new kids can't get through the door without us knowing."

"I'm going to check anyway," Randolph snapped.

"You just don't have any more good cards, probably," Howard mumbled under his breath.

"I'll be back in a minute and don't look at my cards," Randolph warned. "I'll know if you did."

"Sure, sure," Howard replied with a shrug. "You go chase some shadows and I'll wait here. If you don't come back or you see anything, give a holler and I'll come in guns blazing."

Randolph snorted. "You'd be worse than anything out there. With my luck, you'd shoot me by mistake," he retorted, stepping out of the room.

"I'm still a better shot than Alex," Howard called out.

Dust pressed back against the wall as Randolph walked by him. He held his breath when Randolph paused for a moment and swept his hand out. A shiver ran through Dust's body when he felt Randolph's hand passing through him.

"I'm feeling ghosts now," Randolph muttered under his breath before he turned and climbed the steps to the top where the cars were parked.

Dust followed him, taking care to stay far enough behind so that Randolph couldn't touch him again. The strain of being faded for so long was pulling at him, but he needed to see what was going on before he went topside. Randolph doubled checked to make sure the door was locked before he shrugged and turned to retrace his steps. Dust pressed his body as close as he could to the wall as Randolph walked past him, this time not hesitating when he did.

Swallowing, Dust climbed up the stairs and passed through the upper doorway. He made sure the large storage area was empty before he reformed. Pulling the car keys out of his pocket, he unlocked the door to their car and climbed inside.

A sigh of pleasure burst through him as he opened a can of apricots and devoured it. Three cans of fruit, four bags of chips, and two candy bars later, he could feel the power buzzing inside him. Turning back around, he reached into another bag that held several boxes of energy bars. He ripped two of them open and stuffed as many of the bars into his pockets as he could for Josie.

Dust climbed out of the car and quietly closed the door again and locked it. He started to turn when the feeling that had shaken him earlier, hit him again. Turning back toward the entrance to the large curved hanger that doubled as a garage, he stared at the thick, metal doors.

For a moment, he could almost see the dark shadow and glowing red eyes of the devil dog from the town. A frown creased his brow as he tried to focus on where the feeling was coming from. It was still faint, but it ran down his spine like fingernails on a chalkboard. It was coming.

Stumbling backwards, Dust shook his head when the feeling faded again. He had never felt anything like this before. It was almost like when Josie had known he was there even though she couldn't see him. Glancing at the doors once more, Dust felt the urge, more than ever, to get Sammy, Todd, and now Josie, as far away from here as possible.

\.\.*

Dust passed through the door once again. He didn't pause to listen to Randolph and Howard this time, but continued down the spiraling maze deeper and deeper into the silo until he reached the very bottom where Josie was being held.

He passed through the door with a growing urgency to get back to his room. He would have followed that urge if it wasn't for the fact he knew that Josie was in desperate need of something to eat. He solidified into his corporal body as soon as he passed through the door.

"Dust!" Josie whispered, rising up from her pallet on the floor. "I didn't imagine you, you are real!"

"Yes, I'm real," Dust replied, reaching into his pockets and pulling out the energy bars. "I can't stay, but I wanted to give you these. Hide what you don't eat, including the wrappers. We need to get out of here. There's something going on. I'm not sure what it is, but I can feel it."

"Me, too," Josie said, tearing open one of the energy bars and biting into it with a soft groan before she looked up at him. "Thank you."

Dust's gaze softened at the genuine look of appreciation in Josie's eyes. It was hard to believe that he was not alone any more. It was even harder to believe that there were others similar to him.

"Try to ration them," he suggested with a nod of his head as he dropped a small pile of twenty of the vitamin-packed bars onto the mattress. "I'll come for you when we are ready to go."

Josie nodded. "Dust, I don't like the feeling I'm getting. Whatever is causing it is dangerous."

Dust stared back at Josie for a moment before he jerked his head in agreement. He could feel the danger. Turning, he faded and quickly ran up the stairwell to the third level. His gaze widened when he saw Beau opening the door to his room. Randolph was standing outside of it. They were talking too low for him to hear, but he knew it was about him when Beau glanced at the room he and Todd had been given.

He rushed across, moving in the parallel direction when both men started toward his room. He passed through the door and reformed. Moving as quietly as he could, he pulled his shirt off and tossed it on the floor before scrambling onto his cot and pulling the covers over his lower half.

"Dust?" Todd murmured in a sleepy voice.

"Shush, Todd. Pretend you're asleep," Dust ordered in a soft whisper. "We've got company."

Todd blinked a couple of times before he nodded and rolled over so his back was to the door. Dust watched as Todd closed his eyes again and slowly breathed in and out. He closed his own eyes as the sound of the lock being turned echoed unusually loud in the room before the door opened.

"They're both in here," Beau said, flashing a light over both beds.

Randolph's muttered curse almost pulled a smile from Dust. Rolling onto his side, he released a soft snore for good measure. A few seconds later, the door closed again and he heard the lock click back into place.

Cracking his eyelids, he stared down at Todd. A huge grin curved the boy's lips as he stared silently up at Dust. Unable to keep his own amusement hidden, Dust grinned back. Now, to get some rest so he could figure out the best way to get everyone out without getting killed.

..*

The Alpha laid on the ground outside of the huge metal dome two days later. Her stomach was full and she could feel the power coursing through her. Her gaze swept over the remaining nine devil dogs as she brushed her tongue over her teeth.

Attack, her Beta's thoughts whispered through her mind.

Turning her attention to the large male, her gaze swept over him and she felt her body respond to his stare. Her heat was coming. She forced the feeling down, instead focusing on his statement.

Not yet, she responded, gazing back at the half buried structure. *When darkness falls, we will attack.*

She was satisfied when he bowed his head to her. If he had questioned her or snarled in disfavor, she would have to consider promoting another one of the pack to his position. She would not tolerate any of them thinking they should challenge her decisions.

Pleased with his behavior, she released a small snarl and a command as she rose to her feet. Perhaps she should not resist the heat building inside her, she thought as she moved her tail to the side. She nipped at the Beta as he came around behind her. Bracing herself, she allowed him to mount her. Her mind cleared and she let her body relax under the weight of the male.

Tonight, she thought as the male above her grunted with need. *Tonight I will feast on a different flesh. One that will give me more power.*

***

Dust paused as he scrubbed the floor in the kitchen. He looked around the room with a frown. He had felt a shift in the air. Bowing his head again, he focused on the floor in front of him. He was slowly running the mop back and forth over the concrete when Beau walked into the room.

"I'm assigning you another task," Beau stated.

Dust looked up and nodded. The last two days, he, Todd, and Sammy had seldom been in the same room together. In fact, breakfast and dinner were the only two times he had been permitted to see them. The rest of the day they had each been assigned chores in different areas of the complex.

"What do you need me to do?" Dust finally asked when Beau didn't continue.

"We are moving more of the boxes of supplies in the hanger down to the missile storage. I'll need you to help Randolph, Alex, and Howard with that," Beau said.

"Okay," Dust replied and turned to place the mop into the bucket of dirty water.

"I also want you to empty out the car you came in. All the supplies will be added to what we have," Beau added.

Dust's mouth tightened for a moment, but something told him to hold his tongue. He decided he would focus on the first task at hand before resisting the second. It was hard to plan an escape if he couldn't talk to Sammy. She had slipped him a note last night at dinner to warn him that Maria had moved into her room with her. What was even more disturbing was that he had come back last night to discover that Todd had been moved out of his room and into Howard's.

"Why did you move Todd?" Dust asked.

Beau raised an eyebrow at Dust's sudden question. "Because I thought it best," the older man responded.

"Why?" Dust asked, releasing the handle of the mop and stepping closer to Beau. "He should be with either me or Sammy, not Howard. I don't want him there."

Beau stiffened and looked Dust in the eye. "Listen, boy," he began as his eyes narrowed in warning. "I make the decisions here. I don't give a damn about what you want or don't want. The boy stays with Howard."

Dust shook his head. "And if I don't agree with your decisions?" He asked in a quiet voice. "I promised to protect him and Sammy. I can't do that if they aren't near me."

"You don't have to worry about that any more," Beau responded in a hard tone. "If you don't agree, get over it. I told you when you came, I make the rules and my rules are law here. Howard will watch over Todd. And the girl…."

Dust felt a sense of panic when he heard Beau's voice fade. A vision of Sammy swept into his mind at the same time as Randolph's words from the other night suddenly resonated through him.

"I want the girl," repeated itself over and over until Dust had to shake his head to break it.

"What about Sammy?" Dust asked in a husky voice.

Beau glanced at Dust before he looked away. "She's not your problem any longer. Randolph will be overseeing her from now on," Beau explained. "If you are finished here, report upstairs to Alex."

Dust watched Beau turn away and walk out of the room. His fingers curled and he could feel the sparks of power tingling in his palms. Drawing in several deep, steadying breaths, he slowly relaxed. Tonight they would escape. Josie was stronger than she had been. She still needed more food, but they didn't have much choice. He wouldn't let Beau isolate him from Todd and Sammy and he sure as hell wouldn't let Randolph oversee Sammy in any way, shape, or form.

Turning, he rummaged through the drawers in the kitchen until he found a piece of paper and a pencil. He wrote the word 'TONIGHT' in capital letters on two sections and ripped it apart. He would give them to Sammy and Todd at dinner, if not sooner. Replacing the pencil, he shoved the notes into his pocket before dumping the pail of dirty water down the drain and replacing it in the storage area.

Dust wiped his hands down the sides of his pants. The best thing for him to do was to pretend that everything was normal. He would do his chores, but his mind was already focused on how he was going to get Sammy and the others out tonight – in one piece.

Chapter 14

Prisoner:

Dust wiped the sweat off of his brow as he set the last box down in the lower missile bay now being used for storage. The domed hanger upstairs was bare of items except for the vehicles. He hadn't mentioned anything to Randolph or the others about the car that he, Sammy, and Todd had arrived in.

"One more thing and we'll be done," Randolph said, wiping his hands down his pants. A sinking feeling built in Dust's stomach when he glanced at him. "The car you came in is locked. Give me the keys."

Dust's lips tightened and he straightened his shoulders. Randolph was four years older than he was, two inches taller, and outweighed him by at least twenty pounds. He watched warily as the other two men turned to look at him. Drawing in a deep breath, he stared back at Randolph.

"No," Dust said in a quiet voice. "Those supplies belong to Sammy, Todd, and me."

Randolph jerked his head at Howard and Alex. "Not anymore, it's ours," he replied, curling his fingers back and forth.

Dust kept his gaze on Randolph. The odds weren't good, but he knew that he couldn't risk losing the supplies they had found. Shaking his head, he breathed in and out to keep the power building inside him under control. He could feel it fighting to rise up as the primitive urge to fight or flee swept through him.

"No," Dust repeated. "We haven't decided if we are staying or not."

"Oh, you're staying, at least the girl and the kid are," Howard chuckled.

Randolph shot Howard an angry glare. "Shut up, Howard," he snapped. "Give me the keys, Dust. You've been using our supplies, now it's time that you pay up."

Dust lifted his chin and stared stubbornly back at the three other men. His fingers curled into a fist. He could feel the tingling building. If they knew what he could do, it could have serious repercussions on Sammy and Todd.

"We've paid for the meager helpings you've fed us with work. If we decide to stay, then I'll unlock the car, but until we decide, it stays in the car," Dust argued.

"That's not…," Randolph started to say when Beau interrupted him.

"That will be fine," Beau said from behind him.

Dust turned and looked suspiciously at the older man. Beau was standing in the doorway to the former missile launch staring at him. Dust backed up when he saw Beau nod to the other three men.

"But, Beau, you said…," Howard started before biting off a curse when Randolph hit him in the arm.

"What did you say?" Dust asked warily.

Beau's lips tightened in aggravation. "Once you decide you want to stay, then we'll get the stuff out of the car. It doesn't really matter if it is stored topside or down here," he replied with a shrug. "We'll be making another run at the beginning of the week anyway."

Dust started to relax. "Where do you go?" He asked curiously.

"A hundred miles or more in any one direction," Beau said. "It's time for dinner. Stella said for us to get up there if we want to eat."

Dust jerked to the side when Randolph knocked into him as he walked by. He watched warily as Alex and Howard followed Randolph. The three men passed Beau and headed back up the staircase. Dust started forward to follow them, but stopped when Beau reached out and touched his arm.

"Dust, I won't warn you again. My word is law down here. Do you understand," Beau warned in a soft voice.

Dust nodded. Stepping around the man, he continued up the stairs, conscious of the fact that Beau was just a few feet behind him. More than ever, the sense that it was time to move on was pushing at him. Tonight, they would leave.

..*

Sammy glanced at him when he came into the dining area. He shot her a look of warning before he turned his eyes away. Walking over to the pan of water set up for them to wash their hands, he quickly cleaned them. Randolph and the others were already seated at the long table. The only ones missing were him and Beau – and Josie, of course.

"Stella, say the prayer," Beau ordered as he sat down at the head of the table.

Dust kept his head bowed, but his eyes open as Stella mumbled a few words. He slipped his hand into his pocket to retrieve the two notes he had written earlier. He'd have to figure out a way to get them to Sammy and Todd before they disappeared for the night.

They all ate in silence. Meals never took long as the portions were kept to a minimum. Dust felt his stomach twist and growl. He glanced up when he heard one of the children giggle. He winked at the little boy.

"Carter, behave," Stella replied sternly.

"Yes, ma'am," Carter mumbled, looking down at his plate.

Dust's gaze moved to Sammy when he heard her release a frustrated breath. He frowned when he saw a slight discoloration on her right cheek as she pushed her hair back. A dark scowl creased his brow when he saw it was the beginnings of a bruise.

"Who hit you?" Dust asked bluntly, breaking the silence.

"Dust!" Beau spoke in a sharp tone, staring at him.

Dust ignored Beau. "Who hit you, Sammy?" He demanded, clenching his fists.

Sammy glanced at Stella before turning back to Dust. He caught the resentful glare. Rising out of his seat, he stared at Stella.

"Dust, it's okay," Sammy muttered, rising as well.

"No, it's not okay. I promised to protect you," Dust said through gritted teeth. "No one should hit you… Ever!"

"Sit down!" Beau ordered, resting his palms on the table. "Now!"

Dust turned his glare on Beau. "We're leaving, now," Dust said, curling his fingers into a fist. "Come on, Sammy. Todd, you stay close to your sister."

Dust pushed his chair back and turned toward the door. He stiffened when he saw Beau step in front of it. His jaw worked back and forth.

"I warned you, Dust," Beau said. "You're right, it's time for you to leave. You can take the boy with you. We don't need him, but the girl stays."

"No," Sammy gasped, trying to break away from where Stella and Randolph had her pinned between them. "If they go, so do I."

Beau shook his head. "There are enough males here, but we need more women," he stated in a blunt tone.

"Why?" Sammy gasped.

"You are the future, Sammy," Beau replied with a glance in her direction. "Stella is getting too old to have any more babies, which leaves Maria. There are more men than women. While I can control my needs, the others are growing impatient for some younger company."

"I've already claimed dibs on her, Beau," Randolph interjected loudly.

Beau's mouth tightened. "I already told you she could be yours, but you'll have to share until we can find more women," he snapped.

Dust shook his head. "You're all crazy," he whispered, glancing around the room.

"It's called survival, boy," Beau said with a shake of his head. "Take Sammy down to her room, Randolph. Howard, grab the boy. You need to understand that resources are limited, Dust."

"Let me go," Sammy shouted in anger.

Dust turned, his eyes glittered with fury to see Randolph with his arms wrapped around Sammy. Todd kicked Howard in the shin and dropped down under the table to scramble out of Howard's reach when he cursed and let go of him. Dust jumped up onto the table, kicking dishes out of his way as he focused on freeing Sammy. Randolph saw him coming and thrust her into Stella's arms just a fraction of a second before Dust jumped.

Mass chaos exploded through the room. Maria grabbed the younger children and pulled them out of the room. Sammy struck out at Stella, catching the older woman in the chest and arm as she fought to break free. Alex twisted around the table to help Randolph while Howard tried to grab Todd.

Dust sensed Alex before he actually saw him. He had his hands wrapped around Randolph's wrists to keep him from striking him. Raising up his left leg, he kicked out. The blow struck Alex in the groin, knocking him to his knees. Unfortunately, it also knocked Dust off balance. Randolph took advantage of it and rolled so that he was now on top of Dust.

"Stop!" Beau shouted. "Stop, or I'll kill the boy."

Dust froze, his gaze locked on Randolph's eyes before he forced them away to look at where Beau was standing with a pistol pressed against Todd's temple. Todd's whimper echoed through the suddenly silent room.

"Randolph, let him go," Beau ordered.

Randolph pushed upward. Dust winced when Randolph struck him in the mouth. He watched warily as Randolph wiped his own mouth where Dust had gotten a lucky blow. Sitting up, he slowly rose to his feet.

"Dust," Sammy whispered, coming to stand next to him.

Dust slipped his hand into Sammy's trembling one and squeezed it in reassurance. His gaze remained locked on Randolph and Beau. He ignored Howard, who climbed to his feet to stand next to Stella.

"Let him go, Beau," Dust demanded.

"Turn around," Beau ordered. "Now, Dust. I won't repeat myself. You and the boy are trouble. I could see it from the first time I saw you."

"I won't leave without Sammy," Dust responded, gently tugging Sammy behind him.

Beau shook his head. "You still think you can do what you want," he chuckled, twisting Todd's arm when Todd started to wiggle. "Be still boy."

"Leave my brother alone," Sammy angrily snapped. "He's just a little boy."

"On the count of three, I put a bullet in his head if you don't turn around and put your hands behind your back," Beau responded. "One."

Dust stared for a second longer before he slowly turned around and put his hands behind his back. The look in other man's eyes told him that he would do it. This was his domain and he would do anything he had to in order to keep it, including killing Todd.

"Dust," Sammy whispered.

"It will be okay, Sammy," Dust muttered. "I won't leave you."

Sammy cried out when Stella came up and wrenched her arm back behind her. Dust started to turn when a wrenching pain exploded through the back of his head. He felt his body falling forward and instinctively tried to protect himself, but a second blow made everything go dark.

I... have to... remember... my... promise, he forced through his mind before he slipped down into the inky blackness.

..*

Dust came awake in stages. His head hurt so bad, that it made him nauseous. It took three tries before he could withstand the dim light shining down from the ceiling. He rolled onto his back, holding back a moan of pain as he tried to figure out where he was. He blinked again when the light was suddenly blocked by a familiar face.

"Jo… Josie," he choked out in confusion. "Where… Where am I?"

Josie gave him a sardonic smile. "Just be thankful they threw you in here with me instead of outside. I guess there has been the mother of all storms raging the last day and a half. On a good note, Randolph said I could torch you if I wanted. I told him if he gave me some food, I'd torch his ass for free as well," she said with a wry smile, sitting back against the pillar. "I think they've given me even less."

"Randolph's like us," Dust commented, looking at Josie. "You know that, don't you?"

Josie chuckled and leaned her head back so she could stare up at the ceiling. "He wishes he was like us," she murmured. "His only 'talent' if you can call it that, is sensing danger."

Dust shook his head. "I saw his eyes. They turned red," he insisted, sitting up with a moan as it throbbed.

"I have six of the bars you brought me last night under the mattress," Josie said with a sigh. "If you are like me, you'll heal faster if you have food."

Dust glanced at her from under his eyelashes. "Yeah, it helps," he muttered, reaching for one of the bars that she had dug out from under the corner of the mattress.

"So, what are we going to do? I heard Beau say the storm should diminished by tonight. They plan on throwing you and some kid named Todd out as soon as it is safe enough to transport you far enough away you can't get back. I have to warn you, though. The last time they said that, it was with a bullet to the head to make sure that none of the others came back here," she informed him.

"We eat all the energy bars that you have," Dust told her around a mouthful of the high protein bars.

"Why?" Josie asked, looking at him suspiciously.

Dust looked at her with a steely gaze, the haze of pain gone as his body felt the fuel of the protein bar coursing through him. He was going to get Todd and Sammy out of here and he was going to need Josie's help. There was no way that any of them could stay here any longer.

"We're leaving here. Tonight," he responded, pushing up off the mattress. "Give me half of the protein bars and you eat the other half. I'm going to need your help."

Josie handed him two more bars and kept three of them for her. She ripped the wrapper off of one and bit into it. Dust quickly consumed the other two bars.

"Can I toast their asses?" Josie asked as she started eating the second bar.

"Yes, but not Marie or the kids," Dust instructed before he paused and looked at her. "Is Beau really your dad?"

Josie's lips tightened and she looked away. "Not anymore," she whispered, staring at the dark marks from her first few days down here before looking back at him. "How are we going to get out of here?"

"You leave that to me," Dust replied with a determined grin.

Chapter 15

Escape:

Dust rolled his head on his shoulders as he rose to his feet. He glanced down at Josie and nodded to the chains. His brow creased in a frown as he tried to think of a way to get them off of her.

"We need to get those off of you," he said. "Do you know where Beau keeps the key?"

Josie shrugged. "Probably in his room," she replied. "I could melt them off, but it would use up the little bit of energy that I have."

Dust shook his head. "I'll get the key," he reassured her. "I need to find out where Todd and Sammy are. We're not leaving without them."

"That's fine with me," Josie remarked. "You just make sure you don't leave me behind either."

Dust chuckled and shook his head. "No way," he replied with a grin. "You might be handy to have around."

Josie snorted. "You just melt my heart, Dust," she replied sarcastically. "So, what is the plan?"

Dust looked at the door. "I'm going to go find the key to the locks on your wrists, let Sammy and Todd know we are busting out of here, and cause a little distraction to keep the others busy," he replied, taking a step toward the door.

"What kind of distraction?" Josie asked, pulling the chains around the pillar as she followed him.

Dust glanced over his shoulder and shrugged. "I don't know, but you'll know it when it happens," he replied.

"Dust," Josie said, reaching out and touching his arm when he started forward again.

"Yeah?" Dust muttered, looking at her.

"Thank you," she whispered, her gaze softening in the dim light. "Thank you for not leaving me here to rot."

Dust nodded before he focused. Fading, he passed through the thick metal door. He solidified on the other side and hurried up the steps, pausing when he reached the section above. He glanced around the doorway. Stella sat in a chair near the lamp, sewing, while Maria sat with the other children. He didn't see Sammy or Todd.

"She's finally grown quiet. I hope she is asleep," Maria commented.

Stella glanced at the door to Sammy's room. "If not, I'll have Randolph take her up to his room. That'll quiet her down," the older woman remarked.

"She's still young," Maria murmured in protest.

Stella gave Maria a sharp look. "She's old enough, Maria," she snapped. "Don't go feeling sorry for her. The men have treated us all well. We know what needs to be done to keep the peace."

Maria ducked her head and nodded. "Yes," she whispered.

Dust had heard enough. His lips tightened in determination. Fading again, he moved through the room, making sure he kept a good distance from Stella and Maria. After Josie shared with him that others like him could sense the presence of those that were different, and discovering Randolph was more than what he appeared, he didn't want to take a chance of getting caught.

He slipped by the women and into Sammy's room. A grin curved his lips when he saw that she had moved the bed in front of the door so it couldn't be opened. Sammy's pale face shone in the light of a dim lamp near the bed. Dust reformed and stepped up to the bed. He leaned down and whispered her name.

His hand shot out to cover her mouth when it looked like she was going to scream. Her eyes widened when she saw him and her arms rose to wrap tightly around his neck. The move knocked him off balance and he fell over her.

"I thought they had killed you," she whispered in a broken voice against his neck. "I thought you were dead."

Dust clumsily pulled Sammy into his arms and rested against her soft form, surprised by the warmth that swept through him. He lowered his head and buried his face against her neck, breathing in her familiar scent. A grin curved his lips when her arms tightened around him.

"I guess you missed me, huh?" He whispered.

He felt the shudder that ran through her body and his smile died. He could also feel the dampness of her tears. Pulling back, he looked down at her.

"I told you I wouldn't leave you," he murmured, reaching up to brush her hair back from her face. "Do you know where Todd is?"

Sammy sniffed and nodded. "They were going to keep him with Howard, but Howard complained about Todd's crying so they put him back in your old room," she said. "I heard Maria and Stella talking about it a little while ago. Where were you? I heard them say they were going to take you away."

"They were, but there is a storm and they couldn't do it without getting themselves killed, too," Dust murmured. "They put me down below with a girl named Josie. She's sort of like me, but different. I promised to help her escape, too."

"What are we going to do?" Sammy asked, sitting up when Dust moved back to sit on the bed.

Dust gently lifted her hand and threaded his fingers through hers. He had been so afraid that Randolph had hurt her. A shudder went through his body. He would have killed Randolph, Beau, Howard, and Alex if they had touched Sammy.

"We're getting out of here tonight," he said with determination. "I've got to find the keys to the locks holding Josie. I'll release her and come back for you and Todd."

"But, what about Beau and the others?" She asked, biting her lip. "I need a weapon of some kind."

Dust smiled. "There are some really nice bows and arrows in the room where the weapons are. I'll bring you some. I'll create a distraction while you, Todd, and Josie make your way up to the car. Here, take these." He quickly pulled the car key out of his pocket and handed it to her. "Don't wait for me. You get out of here. I'll find you if we get separated."

Sammy's lips tightened. "I won't leave you here, Dust," she whispered in a fierce tone.

Dust smiled and lifted his hand to cup her cheek. Unable to resist, he leaned forward and brushed his lips lightly across her stiff ones. Another shudder ran through his body when he felt her relax against him and return the kiss with a hesitant one of her own.

"Just get to the car," he ordered in a soft, firm voice. "Josie will help you."

Sammy's eyes glittered with tears for a moment before she blinked them away and nodded. "I'll be ready," she promised.

Dust pressed another kiss to her lips, this time a little harder before he stood up. He glanced at her one more time before he faded. He would need to find some food first. He was using too much energy for the small amount he had consumed.

Passing through the room again, he made his way up to the next level. He glanced around the room, breathing a sigh of relief when all he saw was Howard sitting at a table on the far side playing Solitaire. This would have been more difficult if it had been Randolph.

He quickly passed through the wall into the small bedroom. Todd was curled up on the cot. His eyes were red and he was sniffing. Dust rematerialized next to the young boy.

"Dust! I knew you'd come back if you were alive," Todd exclaimed in a hushed voice.

Dust barely had time to catch Todd when the boy threw his arms around him. He winced when Todd's knee caught him in the ribs. Still, he didn't complain. He would never complain about having Todd and Sammy, and now Josie, in his life. For so long, he had felt all alone. They were his family now and he would do everything he could to protect them.

"Hey, is that stash of food I brought down here still under the bed?" Dust asked in a husky voice.

Todd released him and wiped his arm across his nose. Dust saw him nod and grinned back at Todd. He held a finger up to his lips as he quietly moved to the corner cot.

Reaching under it, he pulled a small bag of canned fruit, soda, and breakfast bars out from under it. Mindful that Josie would need more food, he quickly ate half of the supplies. His eyes closed as he felt the energy pulse through him.

"I thought you were dead," Todd whispered, coming to kneel beside him. "They won't let me see Sammy, either."

"I know. Sammy thought I was dead, too, but I'm not," Dust replied around a mouthful of peaches. "I'm going to get you guys out. I've got to release

Josie first, then I'm going to cause a distraction. I want you to stay close to Josie and Sammy, you hear me?"

Todd's face wrinkled in confusion. "Who's Josie?" He asked.

Dust reached out and ruffled Todd's shaggy hair. "She's like me, but in a different way. They are holding her prisoner, too. She's going to bust out of here with us," he explained, drinking the last of the heavy syrup. "I need you to be ready to run faster than you've ever run before."

"I will," Todd promised.

"Good. I've got to go, but I'll be back," Dust said, standing. "Just be ready."

He didn't wait to hear Todd's response. The energy was coursing through his body. Picking up the bag containing the remaining food, he dissolved. He wished he could do this with other people, but he couldn't. He could just do it with inanimate objects.

He passed through the walls until he came to Beau's room. It was empty. They were probably all upstairs in the first room or kitchen area.

The room was spotless. It contained a full-size bed, a chair, a nightstand, and a tall chest of drawers against the back wall. The walls were bare except for a single picture. Walking over to it, his eyes widened when he saw a picture of Beau, a small, red-haired older woman that must have been Josie's mom, Josie, and Randolph standing in front of a stone tower that he recognized from his one trip to the Grand Canyon.

He was so fascinated by the picture, he almost missed the key hanging by a string on the wall next to it. A grin curved his lips. This was almost too easy! Reaching out, he grabbed the string and turned. Now, to return to Josie and start the escape. He decided he would draw the guys down to the lower section and lock them in. Maria or Stella could release them, but by the time they did, he planned to be long gone with Todd, Sammy, and Josie. He just needed to clear the way first.

Fading again, he quickly retraced his steps down to the lower level. He reappeared just before he reached the door. He would need to open it. Setting the bag down on the ground, he turned the wheel of the locking mechanism and pulled the door open.

"I'm back," Dust replied with a grin when he saw Josie leaning back against the pillar.

"I thought you were going to cause a distraction?" She remarked with a raised eyebrow.

"After you are free," Dust reminded her as he lifted the bag he brought. "I thought you might like to recharge some."

Josie's eyes glittered with glee. "You have no idea," she muttered, reaching for the bag. "All sugar!" She laughed, lifting her gaze to his face. "There is going to be fireworks tonight!"

Dust shook his head. "Just don't torch Sammy, Todd, or me," he retorted. "Eat. I'll leave the door cracked. Make sure you leave it open. I'm hoping to lure the men down here and lock them in."

"What about Stella and Maria?" Josie asked with glittering eyes.

"I wouldn't mind locking Stella in here, as well," Dust replied with a hard edge to his voice. "She hit Sammy. Maria isn't so bad, and she needs to be there for the other kids."

Josie reluctantly nodded. She was eating as fast as she could. A loud burp escaped her when she drank half a can of soda without stopping. She grinned at Dust's look of amusement.

"Sorry," she replied before finishing the other half. "Oh, that feels so good," she whispered, closing her eyes for a moment.

Dust knew exactly what she was feeling – the rush from the energy. It was addicting. He waited until she opened her eyes before speaking again. When she did, her eyes were glowing with a reddish-yellow flame.

"We need weapons," he said, touching her arm. "I also need your help protecting Sammy and Todd."

"You've got it," Josie murmured, lifting her hand and uncurling her fingers; small flames danced from the ends of them. "I'll get Sammy. You go get Todd."

"Josie," Dust started to say in warning, stopping when she shook her head.

"Dad won't fall for your trick, Dust. He'll hurt Sammy or Todd if he thinks it will keep you in line," she said.

"How do you know?" Dust asked with a frown.

"Because I saw him do that with my mom," Josie replied. "Randolph is just like him. You need to get Todd and get to the weapons. I'll get Sammy."

"What about Stella and Maria?" Dust demanded.

"Leave them to me," Josie replied. "I won't hurt Maria or the kids, but I'm not making any promises about Stella."

Dust didn't like it, but he felt like he didn't have much choice. He knew Josie was right. He had no doubt that Beau would have killed Todd a few days ago if he hadn't quit fighting. He also didn't know what type of powers Randolph had. If they were anything like Josie's, then they would be in trouble.

Reaching into his pocket, he removed the key he had taken and unlocked the twin locks of the wrist cuffs. A dark scowl crossed his face when he saw the bruises and scars from old cuts where the metal had dug into Josie's flesh. His head jerked up when he felt Josie's warm fingertips touch his jaw.

"You are a pretty amazing guy, Dust," Josie whispered, leaning in to brush her lips against his. "Don't change."

Dust stared at Josie for a moment before he stepped back. With a nod, he turned back toward the door. His mind swirling with thoughts. Shaking his head, he focused on the most important one, escape.

"Give me a five minute head start. I want to get the weapons first, before I get Todd," he ordered.

"Time is ticking away," Josie said with a grin. "You'd better be ready to leave, because I'm not staying here another night."

Dust nodded and headed out the door. He didn't fade until he reached the level above. He hurried up the stairs, taking them two at a time. His steps slowed when he neared the kitchen. He could hear men's voices. It was Beau and Randolph. That meant that Alex must be in the upper room near the entrance.

He swept past the entrance and into the locked storage room containing all the weapons. Reforming, he grabbed a bow that he thought Sammy would like and an assortment of arrows. He didn't know much about them and hoped that it was one she could use. He ignored the guns. He could shoot one, but he'd never been very good.

He faded again, hesitating for a moment. If he could knock Alex out, then their way up the stairs would be clear. The problem was he didn't have enough time before Josie went to free Sammy. A soft curse burst from his lips and he shook his head. He'd have to deal with Alex on the way out.

Turning back the way he came, he ran back down the long corridor. A shiver went through him when he passed the kitchen and heard a loud curse. He had forgotten about Randolph for a second. Disappearing around the curve, he could hear Randolph telling Beau that something was wrong.

"I'm telling you, he's free… Shit, so is Josie," Randolph yelled.

"Get the boy," Beau's order echoed behind Dust.

Josie's warning flashed through Dust's mind. She was right, Beau would use Todd, even kill him, to stop them. Dust burst into the lower section and rushed toward Howard, materializing seconds before he reached him. Howard had started to rise out of his chair when he heard Beau and Randolph shouting.

Dust swung out with the end of the bow, catching Howard in the jaw with the tip of it. Surprise widened Howard's eyes before they rolled back in his head and he collapsed. Dust didn't wait. Turning, he ran for Todd's room, hitting the door with his shoulder and breaking the lock.

"Come on," he ordered, reaching for Todd with his free hand.

Todd gazed at him with wide eyes and nodded, grabbing Dust's outstretched palm. Together, they ran for the opened doorway. The sound of running feet echoed behind them. Dust turned in time to see a bright flash of light coming from the lower section. A moment later, Sammy and Josie appeared around the curve.

"We've got to get out of here," Josie snapped. "Follow me!"

Dust started in surprise when Josie hurried back into the area where the men slept. He glanced at Sammy when she reached for the bow in his hand. He quickly released it and handed the bow to her before shrugging the quiver of arrows off his shoulder.

"Where are you going?" Dust demanded when Josie kicked in the door to Beau's room.

"We can't go up and out," Josie said. "They'll have blocked it and I don't know about those two, but I can't go through walls and doors the way you can."

"Then where are we going?" He asked again in frustration.

Josie glanced over her shoulder as she gripped the tall chest of drawers and pulled it away from the wall.

A small door was behind it. She grinned as she opened it.

"Dad owned this place before I was born. I spent my whole life running around exploring it," she said as she pushed the door open. "He seems to have forgotten that. This leads down to the missile storage."

"The only way out of that is through the missile doors. According to Beau, those weigh in at over seventy tons," Dust pointed out, waving for Todd and Sammy to go first.

"Yes, but there is another way that I hope Dad doesn't know about," Josie replied in a quiet voice.

Dust didn't say anything. He heard the men slow and stop. While they thought Dust might not be too much of a threat, they knew that Josie was and were keeping their distance.

The door led to a wider corridor that had been blocked off. It was short and had probably been a maintenance access at one time. At the end, there was a long ladder that led down a short way before another tunnel opened up. Dust glanced behind him, a growing sense of danger causing his hair to stand up on the back of his neck. It was more than just Beau and Randolph, there was something else, something darker. Once again, the feeling that he was being hunted coursed through him. Shaking his head, he turned and stepped onto the ladder.

It had to be because of the men, he thought.

***

The Alpha female rose to her feet and stretched. She stepped out of the culvert that she and her pack had sought refuge in. She turned when she felt her Beta step up beside her. The storm was finally over.

The fragrant scent of torn earth surrounded them. There had been no rain with this storm. Just the odd green lightning that she remembered from her awakening and the savage wind that swirled in massive circles, destroying everything in its path.

She had wanted to attack several nights ago, but the sudden storm forced her and her pack to seek shelter away from where the dome structure was located. With a low snarl, she ordered her Beta to get the others ready.

Tonight, she thought as she trotted out from the cover of the culvert where the slightest scent of gas still clung to the ground.

This was where the creature she hunted had stopped. She knew where they were going now and it didn't take long for her to reach her destination. She could feel the pull of the creature, it was stronger this time. The others in her pack soon caught up with her.

Before long, she stood outside of the metal dome once again. With a growl, she snapped for her Beta to wait for her. Trotting down the slope, she paused outside of the metal building.

Focusing, she felt her front claws lengthen. Rising up on her hindquarters, she raked the metal, piercing it and slowly ripping it back. She did it three times until she was satisfied that her pack could pass through it.

Once inside, she moved between the vehicles. She quickly determined that the area was empty, but the scent of the two-legged beasts was strong, including the one she was seeking. Following the trail, she stopped outside of another door. This one was slightly thicker than the metal siding. She could have ripped through it, but something told her that she needed to proceed with caution.

Focusing again, she faded. She passed through the door and reformed on the other side. Turning, she saw the lock on the door. Rising up again, she leaned forward and gripped the piece of metal between her teeth, pulling it free before pressing her paw down on the handle. The door swung open. Satisfaction coursed through her.

These creatures were not as smart as I thought they might be, she reflected with satisfaction.

Turning, she started down the long flight of stairs. A soft, yellow glow lit the far end. Her Beta and the others moved like dark shadows behind her.

Come, she ordered, turning and stepping down onto the first step. *It is time to hunt.*

Chapter 16

Fight or Die:

Dust tucked his head as he slipped out of the long, narrow tunnel they had just crawled through. He glanced around, surprised that they were in the lower section of the missile bay. There were stacks of boxes all around them. He grinned when he saw Josie look at him with a raised eyebrow.

"I moved most of these here," he said with a shrug, answering her unspoken question.

"Is there food in any of them?" She asked.

"Yep," Dust replied.

Josie rested her hands on her hips when he didn't say anything else. Sammy giggled and Todd grinned. Dust's lips twitched again when Josie lifted a hand and wiggled her fingers for him to finish his sentence.

"The box behind you has some canned goods in it," he added.

Josie turned and frowned. "It says PT," she muttered.

Dust shook his head. "I saw Randolph writing that on it," he explained. "One of the boxes fell open and it was food. He didn't know I saw what he was doing."

"Leave it to my big brother to cover his own ass," Josie scoffed. "He's a chip off the old block, alright. Just like my dad, hard core, bigoted and self-centered."

Dust saw Josie's eyes flash with rage before she opened the top of the box. A low hiss escaped her before her eyes glittered in triumph. She turned toward him and threw a bag containing something white in it. A surprised laugh escaped him when he saw what it was.

"Marshmallows?" Sammy asked, watching as Josie and Dust both ripped a bag open and began stuffing their mouths with the white, sugary concoction. "Can't this wait until after we get out of here? In case you forgot, Beau and the others will be searching for us."

"Let them," Josie growled, holding up a marshmallow. "Do you know what this is?"

"Sugar?" Sammy replied, looking at the small roundish puff with a doubtful expression.

"Sugar," Dust and Josie agreed at the same time.

"It's pure energy," Josie replied, closing her eyes as she felt her body absorbing the sugar. "It is like jet fuel for a freak like us. Randolph was always my dad's favorite, but being different like Dust and me might not save his ass. My dad can be a little unpredictable about certain things."

Josie opened her eyes and stared at them. Dust heard Sammy and Todd's gasp when they saw her eyes glowing with the strange fire that he had seen earlier. Popping another marshmallow into his mouth, he reluctantly closed the bag and tucked it in his shirt.

"Todd, find a bag so we can fill it with the marshmallows," Dust instructed. "Josie, didn't you say you knew of another way out of here that your dad might not know about?"

Josie nodded, holding a marshmallow over her fingers. It wouldn't have been so strange if she wasn't toasting it. Dust fought the urge to tell her to knock it off. He was afraid that she would freak Sammy and Todd out until he heard Todd giggle when Josie held it out to the young boy.

"Thank you," Todd replied with a grin.

"Yes," Josie finally responded. "There is another tunnel. I looked it up once to figure out what it was used for. They needed to use Liquid Nitrogen for the missiles. Of course, they didn't want to store it too close so it was pumped in or whatever through this tunnel. I used it to sneak out at first to go look for food until my jerk of a brother caught me one day roasting a rabbit for dinner and told my dad."

"What happened?" Todd asked curiously, reaching for another marshmallow when Josie held the bag out.

Josie shrugged. "Dad had already eliminated the other people that the strange dust cloud had changed. Personally, I thought he was expecting us to turn into some kind of zombie and start eating on their flesh. I shouldn't have spared either one of them because they were family. They sure as hell didn't treat me like I was family, that's for sure," she explained in a bitter voice. "I came back in and dad tricked me into going down to the lower level. He locked me in there. Three days without food and I was about to go crazy. Ever since that day, he gave me just enough food to stay alive – barely. The last six months have been hell and I don't ever plan on being trapped like that again."

Dust motioned for Sammy and Todd to get behind him. Josie's red hair had begun to whip around her and it looked like her skin and hair were on fire. She was beautiful, but also a little scary, especially when two balls of flames suddenly rose up from the palms of her hands.

"Uh, Josie, you're on fire," Dust pointed out quietly.

Dust waited as she regained control of her emotions. Josie drew in a deep breath and the flames receded. A bitter laugh escaped her and she shook her head as the flames died away.

"Marshmallows," Todd muttered with a shake of his head, staring at the one he still held in his hand. "Wow!"

Sammy gave an uneasy laugh. "We'll bag you some more, but I think you two need to be careful how many you eat," she remarked with an uncomfortable shrug.

"Let's hurry," Dust replied, turning to look up at the ceiling with a frown. "Something's wrong."

Josie turned at the same time. Her lips tightened and the flush that had been on her face, paled. Her lips parted and she glanced back at Dust.

"I feel it, too," Josie said. "It's different. I've felt it when I'm around others like us, but nothing like this before. This is…."

A loud scream cut off her sentence. The sounds of gunshots echoed through the silo. Dust glanced at Sammy and Todd. Sammy had pushed Todd behind her and threaded an arrow into the bow she was holding.

"That was Stella," Josie whispered.

"We can't leave Maria and the children unprotected," Dust muttered, turning to look at Josie. "Take Sammy and Todd and get out of here. Sammy has the keys to the car."

"What about you?" Josie asked with a scowl. "Leave them!"

"The kids don't deserve whatever is there," Dust replied with a shake of his head. "Protect them, Josie. I'm holding you responsible for their safety."

"I can protect Todd and me," Sammy snapped. "We'll wait back at the culvert for you, Dust. You'd better come or we're coming back for you."

Dust nodded. "They are getting closer. Go, Josie!" He ordered, fading as he rushed for the long staircase.

..*

Dust entered the second floor just as a dark shadow slammed into the door to Maria's room. He immediately recognized the devil dogs from the town where he had met Sammy and Todd. Blood coated the floor. Another of the devil dogs was ripping at Stella's still form. A discarded shotgun lay on the ground next to her.

The sound of another scream and shattering wood pulled him back to Maria and the three children pinned in the bedroom. The devil dog was ripping at the door with its claws. Small holes appeared in the door as Maria fired through it again and again. Several struck the devil dog, but that didn't stop its determination to get inside the room. Reforming, Dust lifted his hands and focused.

"Hey!" He yelled, waiting.

Both beasts paused and raised their head to stare at him. Blood dripped from the mouth of the one that had been over Stella. It turned with a low snarl. Backing up to keep his back to the thick concrete wall, he warily watched as the one attacking the door turned at the same time.

Licking his lips, he knew he would only have one shot at killing them. He needed to strike their heart. If he did that, they wouldn't be able to heal. For a moment, he wished Josie was here. The best way to kill them was to toast them.

"That's it. Come on," Dust said.

The sound of his voice seemed to enrage them. In tandem, both beasts leapt at him. Dust knelt down and focused. Twin pulses of electrical charges shot out from his hands, striking the beasts in midair. He faded as their bodies continued in a forward momentum. Rolling, he reformed when they hit the wall, sending another burst through them.

The line of energy cut through the flesh around their necks, decapitating them. He stood and wrinkled his nose in distaste as the heads of the two beasts fell to the side.

Cutting their heads off worked as well, he thought in satisfaction before turning to where Maria and the children were hiding.

"Maria," Dust called out in a quiet voice. "It's me, Dust. Don't shoot, okay? The beasts are dead."

The only sound coming from the room for several long seconds was the muffled sobs of children. In the background, Dust could hear the sound of gunfire. It sounded like it was getting closer.

"Dust," Maria finally whispered in a trembling voice. "Stella…."

Dust walked over to the door. He glanced over his shoulder, thankful that the center pillar hid most of Stella's body from view. Turning back around when he heard the sound of furniture scraping across the floor, he waited for Maria to open the door.

"The kids?" He asked when she peeked out from behind the door before pulling it open wider when she saw him.

"Stella had me barricade myself and the children in the room," Maria explained in a shaky voice. "I heard gunfire."

"Stella's dead," Dust replied, trying to shield the little part that could be seen from the three kids. "I need to get you out of here."

"How… How did you escape?" Maria asked, her gaze darting to the remains of the two devil dogs. Her eyes grew wide with shock. "How did they get in here? Beau swore that nothing could get inside."

"I don't know," Dust replied, ignoring her first question. "Come on. I can feel them getting closer."

"Them? Who? Oh, God!" Maria cried out, stumbling backwards when she caught sight of Stella. "Kathy, Carter, Brian, don't look."

"There are more devil dogs," Dust said in an urgent voice. "There is another way out. Do you know where the culvert under the road is?"

"Ye… Yes," Maria answered, wiping at her eyes. "But, we can't go outside. It's too dangerous."

"It's too dangerous to stay in here," Dust replied, gripping Carter's hand. "Carry the girl. I need to be able to fight if they come at us."

"But, how will we get by them?" Maria asked in a slightly hysterical tone.

"There is a tunnel that leads up to the surface. It comes out several hundred yards from the silo. I need to get you up to the next level. If you go through Beau's room, there is an access tunnel that will take you to the missile bay. On the far side, there is a ladder that leads up to another tunnel. That is the one that will take you to the surface. I'll help you."

"But… What about the others?" Maria asked when they heard another burst of gunfire.

Dust grimly shook his head. "They will have to be on their own," he said. "You and the kids are my priority."

"Why, Dust?" Maria asked, again.

He could see the doubt and suspicion in her eyes. "Because I'm like them, only different," he said in a quiet voice as he nodded toward the two dead devil dogs. "I won't let the kids suffer. I can't make you go, Maria, but I won't leave the kids here. It is up to you if you want to come with us or stay."

Maria glanced at the two dead beasts before looking back at Dust's steady gaze. With a slight nod, she bent and picked up the little girl that was sucking on her thumb and staring straight ahead with a blank gaze.

Dust released Carter's hand and turned toward the door. Pausing to glance around the corner, he motioned with his head for the small group to follow him. They were halfway up the staircase when he saw a shadow. Holding up his hand, he motioned for Maria and the kids to get back against the wall.

Dust slowly moved up the stairs, keeping his eyes on the beast. He was almost in range when the loud sound of a shotgun echoed through the narrow corridor. The beast staggered backwards, before another blast lifted it up and it collapsed and slid down several steps toward him. Rushing up the steps, he quickly placed his hand over the creature's chest and sent a blast of energy through its heart to make sure it stayed dead.

He glanced up when he heard the sound of a shotgun being pumped. His gaze locked with Alex's dazed one. Blood dripped down the side of the other man's face, the left shoulder of his shirt was torn and the skin underneath was ripped as well.

"Maria," Alex whispered in a hoarse voice.

"She and the kids are safe for the moment," Dust replied, slowly rising to his feet and lifting his hands. "I need to get her out of here."

Alex nodded, half turning when more gunfire rang out. "There are so many of them. One of them, it just disappeared and reappeared," he choked out.

Dust's eyes widened and his mouth tightened. "Can you take Maria and the kids to safety? I'll help the others," he reluctantly said.

"How?" Alex replied, turning back to Dust. "Josie?"

"She's gone, along with Sammy and Todd," Dust replied, taking a step up the stairs. "We don't have much time. The longer we delay, the more likely those things will find us and I can't protect you all."

"How can you fight them? I shoot them, but they just get back up," Alex muttered, stumbling down a step.

"Alex, I can stop them," Dust said in a firm voice, masking his own fear. "But, I can't do that and get Maria and the kids to safety. Josie, Sammy, and Todd are at the culvert where you found us. They are waiting for me. I need you to get Maria and the kids there."

He watched as Alex blinked several times before his eyes cleared and he nodded. Dust quickly explained about the tunnels and how to get out. Within minutes, Alex, Maria, and the three children disappeared through Beau's room.

Swallowing, Dust faded. Moving swiftly up the different levels, he listened for the sounds of gunfire and the snarls of the beasts. It sounded like Beau and the others had retreated to the weapons room.

Dust reached the level where the weapons room and the kitchen were located. He paused when he saw the small group of devil dogs. There were four of them trying to get into the room. Cupping his hands, he focused. He would need to strike them all at once. It was going to take a lot of energy. For a brief moment, he half thought about retreating to eat some of the marshmallows out of the bag he had stuffed into his shirt.

A startled gasp escaped him when he saw two more devil dogs coming down the corridor. One was larger than the other, but it wasn't what captured his attention. No, it was the smaller one that moved as if it was floating across the ground. It paused, staring straight at him. Dust watched in disbelief as it dropped what looked like part of a human hand from its bloody jaws.

He staggered backwards when a wisp of a voice echoed through his mind. It shouldn't be able to see him, but he knew that it could. He jerked back another step, reaching for the wall as he reformed.

Mine, the voice whispered in a long hiss of triumph.

Dust blinked and frowned. It felt like the creature was inside his head. Swallowing, he backed away as the other beasts turned at his sudden appearance. The savage snarl of the larger beast had the group whining and nipping at each other as they fought to listen to commands.

"What are you?" Dust asked in a husky voice, intuitively knowing that it could understand him.

The creature paused and tilted its' head at him. *Like you,* it responded as if unaccustomed to communicating with another.

"No, you aren't," Dust answered in a quiet voice. "I don't kill for pleasure."

The beast looked at the others and snorted before turning her gaze back to Dust. Its mouth curved upward, almost as if it was smiling. The glow in its gaze sent a shiver through Dust.

Power, it replied. *I want your power.*

Dust shook his head again. "It doesn't work that way," he said in a husky voice. "You can't just take my power or someone else's."

Not true, the beast replied, stepping closer. *Give me power.*

"I wouldn't, even if I could," Dust responded, slowly lifting his hands toward the female devil dog. "You kill for pleasure; for power. That is wrong."

An angry snarl escaped the female. Dust knew the exact moment she was going to strike. For a brief moment, it was as if they were one and he could see and feel everything that she was and what she wanted. She wanted power. It was like the hunger of food was to him, she craved it, needed it.

He released a burst of electricity in arcing waves, spreading the energy in long, forked bursts. The enraged female charged at him, fading as she jumped so the burst of energy went through open air instead of her corporeal body. Dust barely had time to fade before she reached him.

A loud gasp escaped him when their bodies collided in a powerful collision, sending them both through the thick concrete wall into the kitchen. Dust threw the female off him, re-materializing for a brief moment to grab the long knife on the cutting board before fading again when she recovered and attacked him again. This time, they fell across the table; locked in a deadly battle as they both reformed, unable to keep their faded form as they fought.

Dust dropped the knife as he wrapped his hands around the neck of the female. Sharp, deadly teeth snapped repeatedly at him. Squeezing, he sent a powerful burst of electricity into the beast. The moment the devil dog jerked back, he faded and dropped through the table. He grunted when he hit the hard floor under him.

Die, she snarled, shaking off the shock.

"Not today," Dust replied, rolling out from under the table and into a crouch.

He kept his gaze locked on the female as another figure appeared in the entrance to the kitchen. She was calling in reinforcements. There was no way he could fight them all. She was the one that was the true threat.

The faint connection he had with her forced him into motion. Springing toward her as the larger black body burst at him, Dust faded as the male jumped at him. He reformed long enough to bury the knife he held in the female's side before fading again and disappearing through the wall. He didn't pause. He was losing blood from the wounds the female's claws had cut into his flesh and using too much energy.

Surging up through the stairway, he passed by two dead devil dogs, killed by his electrical charge, and several wounded ones that were feeding on the dead dogs remains. He staggered, but pushed forward through the upper doors until he reached the garage partition of the silo.

He reformed, stumbling and falling to one knee. His left hand braced him from planting his face into the ground. He lifted his right hand and touched his ripped chest. Warm, sticky blood quickly coated his fingers. Pushing up off the ground, he made his way to one of the large trucks.

Reaching up, he opened the driver's door and pulled himself inside. A quick check showed that the keys were hidden under the seat. He hissed when the skin pulled across his chest. It took him three tries before he was able to push the key into the ignition.

The truck started smoothly and he quickly shifted into reverse. The truck slammed through the second door that was partially closed. He jerked forward when he hit a bank of dirt outside the doors. Shifting the truck into drive, he punched the gas. The tires spun for a moment before it jerked forward.

Dust blinked to clear his vision as he bounced along the rough, dirt and gravel road. He had lost his bag of marshmallows during the fight. With a sigh of resignation, he focused on the road ahead of him and the hope that Josie, Sammy, and Todd had made it out of the silo.

Raising a bloody hand to push the hair that had fallen forward out of his eyes, he glanced in the mirrors. The feeling of rage was slowly growing fainter. He hadn't killed the creature. It was wounded and furious, but alive. Another shiver ran through him when he caught a faint hint of a voice in his head.

Until next time – human, the female's voice hissed.

Chapter 17

The Change:

"Thank you again for everything," Maria murmured in a quiet voice.

"If you see any of the others again, you won't tell them anything, will you?" Josie asked, moving from one foot to the other and staring intently at Alex more than she was Maria.

"No, we won't," Alex said with a grimace. "I doubt that they survived. That one creature...." He shook his head and looked uneasily at Josie before glancing at Dust. "I doubt we'll ever see any of them again."

Dust glanced at Maria and Alex with a frown. "Are you sure you want to split up? You could travel with us," he said in a quiet voice. "What do you plan to do?"

Alex glanced at Maria before he spoke. "We are going to head east. I had some family in North Carolina. I'm hoping some of them may have survived. I... I owe you an apology, Dust. Maria, the kids, and I would all be dead now if not for you. Beau said...."

"Dad said a lot of crap," Josie interrupted in a hard voice.

Dust glanced at Josie. She had the flames glowing in her eyes again. She tended to do that whenever Alex opened his mouth. It had been a battle the last three days to keep her from torching Alex. If the other man owed anyone an apology, it was Josie.

Alex and Maria had decided it was better for them to go off on their own. Neither one of them felt comfortable around him or Josie. While Dust was concerned about their safety, he also knew it was their choice. It was the three small children with Alex and Maria that he was concerned about. Still, they were all probably better off as far away from him as possible. The haunting threat of the female devil dog was burned into his memory.

"Stay together," Dust said, nodding to Alex. "I wish I could give you some advice on how to know if there are any more of those creatures around, but I can't. Just keep your eyes open and try not to move around too much at night if you are out in the open."

"We won't," Alex replied with a stiff nod. "We've got to get going before it gets too much later."

Dust's eyes widened in surprise when Maria stepped forward and gave him a hug. He stood stiffly, not sure of what to do. She quickly released him and stepped back again with a murmur of thanks before she turned and walked to the waiting truck that he had taken from the silo. Several minutes later, only the faint outline of the truck could be seen in the distance.

Dust turned and looked around the small town that they had taken refuge in several days ago. He didn't remember much of the first day. It had taken every ounce of his strength to get to the culvert. His chest had been ripped open by the she-devil's claws.

"How are you feeling?" Sammy asked, staring at him in concern. "You still look pale."

"I'm good," Dust replied with a crooked grin. "Although, I wouldn't object to another bag of marshmallows if we have any."

Sammy shook her head. "We don't," she said with a sigh of regret. "I do have some soda and chips."

Dust nodded. "I'll take the soda," he said, taking a step closer to Sammy when she turned to walk back to the car where Todd was waiting for them. "Did you or any of the others find anything worth salvaging?"

Sammy shook her head. "No," she replied.

"This was one of the towns my dad and brother hit," Josie said with a shrug. "I was with them when they came the first couple of times. They must have come back for more. I don't remember it being this empty when I was here before."

"I think it would be best to head out," Dust suggested. "There were several more towns and we might find some houses along the way that they missed."

"Good luck with that," Josie replied with a snort. "My dad was pretty good about finding stuff."

"How far out did they go, Josie?" Sammy asked, frowning.

Josie shrugged. "I don't know," she said. "Not far at first, but I was locked up the last six months, so who knows. I just know that I am NEVER going underground again!"

Dust watched as Josie raised her face to the sky. Since the fragments of the comet hit the earth, there were never any real sunny days. A layer of clouds covered the sky. The weather was cooler than it had been before. What should be the hottest part of the summer felt more like the beginnings of winter.

"Here you go, Dust," Sammy said, holding out a can of soda.

"Thanks," Dust replied, taking the soda from her. He looked at her when she didn't let go of the can at first. She was studying him with a worried expression. He reached up with his other hand, smoothing back a strand of her dark hair when it blew across her face. "I'm glad you and Todd made it out safely," he said in a husky voice.

"Are you okay? I mean, really," Sammy murmured in a soft voice. "The few times I've seen you hurt, you seemed to heal faster after you ate something. This time it took longer."

Dust glanced down at the soda in his hand. She was right, it had taken longer. Of course, some of the wounds to his chest had been deeper than the other wounds he had suffered. He had also lost a lot of blood.

"I'm fine," he finally said, looking up at her again with a slight smile.

"Can we leave, already?" Josie snapped, glaring back and forth between Sammy and Dust. "I'll drive."

Dust didn't miss the way Sammy's lips tightened into a straight line or the flash of annoyance in her eyes. He heard Todd mumble that it was about time as he crawled across the back seat. Deciding that it would probably be best if he sat next to Todd, he climbed in the back seat and pulled the door closed.

"So, which way do we head?" Josie asked as she climbed into the driver's seat.

"North," Sammy and Dust said at the same time.

"Can I ask why? It seems like it will only be colder up there," Josie asked, glancing over her shoulder at Dust.

"I have family in Portland," Dust said. "I don't know if they are still alive, but I want to find out."

Josie raised an eyebrow before she turned and looked at Sammy. "What about you?" She asked.

Sammy started and half turned in her seat so she could look back at him. Dust could feel her surprise at his admission. He had never told her about his aunt and uncle that lived in Portland. His mom's brother lived there. They had actually visited him and his aunt just the Christmas before the comet struck.

"It's just Todd and me," Sammy finally replied, turning back in her seat. "We have a little over half a tank of gas and two gas cans that are filled. We'll need to keep an eye out for any gas stations we can find. We'll also need more food. At the rate you and Dust are eating, what we have now won't last very long if we don't."

Josie flashed a grin. "I won't need quite as much as I was eating. I'm feeling the energy inside me. Still, you'll appreciate my appetite if we meet any more of those devil dog creatures. I'll be able to roast the lot of them!"

"I just hope we find more marshmallows. They were good the way you toasted them, Josie," Todd commented from the back seat.

"Thanks, Todd," Josie chuckled. "I love being free!"

Dust laughed and tiredly laid his head back against the seat. Lifting the can to his lips, he sipped on the sugary mixture. He could feel the energy slowly coursing through him.

Turning his head, he watched as the landscape flashed by. His mind played back over the battle with the devil dog. Worry tugged at him. Deep down, he knew that he had not seen the last of that creature.

His gaze turned to the back of Sammy's head. He hadn't told her about the strange sensations that had been running through his body since the day of the fight. At first, he had thought it was because of his injuries, but now he wasn't so sure. It felt like his skin was crawling.

There was also the uncontrollable hunger. He had eaten through a third of what had been stored in the car over the last three days. Sammy hadn't tried to stop him, but she had watched him with growing alarm. Josie on the other hand, had been rather blunt when she told him that he needed to slow down until they had a chance to find another town.

The last thing he noticed was it felt like he was still running a fever. By the time he reached Sammy, Todd, and Josie the other night, his skin had felt like he was on fire. He had fallen into the back of the car while Josie drove. Todd had sat in the front seat while Sammy had stayed in the back with him, constantly running a damp cloth over his fevered skin. Alex, Maria, and the kids had followed in the large truck Dust had taken. His fever finally broke late yesterday afternoon. When it did, that was when his appetite had gone crazy.

Now, he was just tired. All he wanted to do was sleep. Turning his head, he rested his forehead against the cool glass and closed his eyes. It felt so good, both the cool glass against his skin and the closing of his eyes. They had a long road ahead of them before they would stop for the night. He would sleep until then, or at least for just a little while, he thought as Sammy and Josie's soft voices washed over him.

..*

Kill one, the female devil dog ordered, glaring up at her Beta with eyes glazed with pain and rage.

The Beta didn't question her order. She would have killed him if he had. Instead, she watched the large male trot over to where the remainder of her pack lay resting. This would be the second one that he would kill for her in the past day. Her hunger was eating at her with an intensity so strong that she was amazed she hadn't killed the rest of the pack.

The sound of fighting drew her attention back to the group. The Beta had picked the weakest of the survivors, but it was still strong. The fight to live was strong inside the devil dog, but it was no match for the larger Beta. Several minutes later, the Beta returned, dragging a limp body clutched between its thick, powerful jaws.

Yes, the She-devil groaned, rising up with difficulty.

She stumbled toward the warm remains of the devil dog. With a ferociousness that belied her feelings of weakness, she fell to the ground and ripped into the flesh of the dead beast. As she ate, she thought of the human who had almost killed her. The pain of the knife wound in her side still throbbed. It had been deep, barely missing her heart.

She snarled when the Beta stepped too close. Snapping her jaws, her eyes blazed a dark, blood-red. She could feel the power coursing through her, as well as something else. Her body felt stiff and achy.

Rising to her feet, she stumbled for a moment before an intense pain swept through her. This was far worse than when she woke that first time. A loud, piercing howl shattered the night air. Twisting, she fell to the ground. Her back and shoulders felt like they were on fire.

The Beta jerked back as she jerked in uncontrollable spasms. In the back of her mind, she could feel his fear. She watched helplessly as he turned and disappeared into the darkness, the remaining devil dogs following him. Her jaws opened and she fought to snarl an order for him to return, but her throat was suddenly paralyzed.

Hot pants escaped her as the skin along her shoulders split open. Her paws curled into the dirt as she desperately tried to hold onto consciousness as waves of pain exploded through her. A low, moan finally broke through the agonizing pain when the pressure inside her finally spilled out onto the ground.

Lifting her head several long minutes later, she tiredly glanced over her shoulder. A sense of triumph and a momentary flash of power swept through her before she laid her head back down. Unable to resist, she wiggled her shoulders. The unfamiliar weight pulled at her.

I am changed, she thought with contentment. *I am stronger. The human cannot escape me now.*

Chapter 18

Rising from the Dust:

"Dust, wake up," a voice said urgently.

A shiver ran through him. He ached all over. He tried to open his eyes, but they felt weighted down. Another shiver shook his body and the sound of someone moaning pulled at him. Was Sammy or Todd hurt? It took several tries before he could get his tired brain to send the right message to his eyelids. He blinked groggily. Bright light streamed through the window of the car. Instead of sitting, he was lying across the back seat of the car. There was a pile of blankets on top of him, but he was still cold.

"Sam... Sammy," he choked out, his throat rough and dry.

"I'm here," Sammy said, leaning over him from where she was kneeling on the floorboard in the back.

"What... Where are we?" He asked, weakly clutching at the blankets. "Why am I so cold?"

Sammy brushed a hand over his forehead. He closed his eyes at the soothing caress of her fingers. His eyelashes lifted when he heard her shift.

"Try to drink this," she said, lifting his head up a little so that she could rest the can against his lips.

The sugary taste of the soda washed over his tongue and down his throat. He fought the urge to sneeze as the fizz tickled his nose. After several sips, she pulled the can away from his lips and gently rested his head back down on the jacket she was using as a pillow.

"What is going on?" He asked.

"You're sick," Josie said, bluntly from the front seat.

"You've been sick for two days," Todd added, looking over the front driver's seat at him. "Sammy said we needed to find a place to stay until you got better."

Dust's gaze moved back to lock with Sammy's worried one. He tried to smile, but it took too much effort. With a sigh, he shifted uncomfortably on the seat. His back felt like it was on fire. He would have understood if it had been his chest, though that still hurt as well.

"Where are we?" He asked faintly.

Sammy looked up to stare out of the door. With a sigh, she glanced back down at Dust. An uncertain smile curved her lips.

"I think we are in Kansas, but I'm not really sure," she admitted.

"How are you feeling?" Josie asked.

Dust turned his head to stare at Josie. "Cold, achy," he mumbled. "I'm not sure what's wrong. My back... It hurts... Burns."

"It could be an infection or something. The devil dogs cut you up pretty bad," Sammy said, biting her lip.

"I told Sammy I could seal the wounds with just a touch, but she wouldn't let me," Josie responded, raising her hand up and focusing until small flames danced on the tips of her fingers.

Dust released a faint chuckle. His fevered gaze glittered with tired amusement. He pulled his hand free of the covers and reached for Sammy's hand.

"Thank you," he said with a small smile. "Something tells me I'd be in a lot worse shape if you hadn't been here."

"She's all talk," Sammy whispered.

"Josie made me some more marshmallows last night," Todd informed him.

Dust's eyes moved back to Josie and he raised an eyebrow at her. Her cheeks flushed and she glanced away. Her lips twisted into a sardonic curve.

"There was only two left. It wasn't like it would have done either one of us much good," Josie retorted, turning back around in her seat and pushing out the passenger side door and sliding out.

He watched as Josie disappeared. Releasing a tired sigh, he looked back at Sammy. Todd had decided to join Josie, so they were alone.

"We found a house," Sammy said. "It was empty. There wasn't any food left, so we think that whoever had lived here might have survived. Josie doesn't think her dad would have made it this far. We're out of gas in the car, too."

Dust tried to push up, wincing when he felt his muscles protest. He gripped the back of the front seat to steady himself when the world spun at a crazy angle. Drawing in deep breaths, he waited until things stood still once more before he spoke.

"Are there any other cars here?" He asked in a husky voice.

Sammy scooted up to sit near his feet. She shook her head. He didn't miss the slight look of worry that crossed her face.

"Don't worry, we'll find a way to move on," he muttered. "Can I have more of the soda?"

"Oh, yeah, here," Sammy said, reaching for the can she had placed on the floorboard. "How are you feeling?"

"A little better," he admitted, taking the can of soda from her and draining it. Almost immediately, he could feel the energy sweeping through him. The cold soda also soothed the soreness in his throat. He leaned back against the seat and gave her a lopsided smile. "That tastes good."

"We have a couple of cans left if you'd like another one," Sammy said.

Dust shook his head. "Not right now," he said, turning his head to look at the small blue and white boarded house.

"We were afraid to move you," Sammy explained, glancing at the house where Josie and Todd were sitting on the front porch talking. "Every time we touched you, you would cry out in pain. Josie and I took turns staying out here with you at night."

Dust reached out and touched Sammy's cheek. A soft flush rose in them and her expression softened. He gently ran his thumb across her skin before his hand dropped back to his lap.

"Do we have any more fruit?" He asked. "I think if I can eat a little bit, I'll be able to move on my own."

Sammy nodded and twisted to grab a couple of cans out of the back. He watched as she removed the lid of the first can and held it out to him. With each bite, he felt stronger.

..*

Five days later, Dust wiped the sweat from his brow. Even though it was growing colder out, he felt warm. He wasn't running a fever like before, he decided it must be because he was jogging. He glanced over his shoulder at the makeshift cart he had constructed. It had four, five gallon gas cans filled to the top. He was pretty proud of his explorations today. It had taken him a bit longer and he had to go a lot farther than he anticipated to find the items, but the journey had been a success.

Turning back around, he gripped the straps and began moving again. He had another four miles to go before he got back to the house where Josie, Sammy, and Todd were waiting for him. They had wanted to go with him, but he was concerned that he might not make it back home before dark. The long, flat road was straight before him and he found it was easier to pull the cart.

His gaze narrowed on a thin wisp of black smoke rising in the distance. Picking up speed, his heart pounded when he realized that the smoke was thicker than he first thought. Panic hit him hard and he moved to the side of the road, releasing the straps of the cart. Running as fast as he could, his eyes remained glued to the thickening blackness.

The heat from earlier returned as he ran. The burning that had been in his back earlier in the week returned. This time, he ignored the excruciating stab of pain. His only concern was for Sammy, Todd, and Josie. He jumped the small ditch, clawing at the ground to get his footing. His hand swung out and he gripped the wooden post, hopping over the tangle of barbed wire. He pushed himself forward over the uneven ground. In the distance he could see the house. In the front yard, there were several vehicles he didn't recognize. One of the trucks was on fire.

Pure rage and fear swept through him when he heard the sound of gunfire. The burning in his back disappeared at the same time as he felt a wave of fire course through him. The world shifted, changing as he faded. His gaze remained on the small group hiding behind the vehicles. The group that was trying to harm Sammy, Todd, and Josie.

..*

Sammy pulled Todd back and held him in her arms as a rain of bullets tore through the wooden siding of the house. She waited until the rounds had stopped before she released Todd. Pushing him toward the couch located against the far wall, she motioned for him to crawl to it.

"Stay down," she whispered, reaching for the bow and arrows that she had grabbed when she saw the four vehicles coming down the road. "Don't move from there unless one of us tells you to."

Todd nodded and scrambled across the floor on all fours. Sammy gripped the bow in her hand and glanced out the window where Josie was standing on the porch. For a moment, Sammy didn't know if she wanted to hug Josie or wring her neck.

The loud explosion of one of the trucks as it rose into the air resonated through the yard and house. Josie had shot a fireball at it. Sammy decided that wringing Josie's neck was probably going to be her first choice, after all. Rolling to the side, Sammy crawled through the living room doorway and into the front bedroom.

"I told you to keep on moving," Josie growled loudly from the porch. "I'm not in the mood to deal with the lot of you."

"That one's got some fire in her, Everett," one of the men yelled.

"I'll show her fire! That was my damn truck she blew up!" The man yelled back. "You messed with the wrong men, she-devil. We'll be sending you back to the hell you escaped from."

Sammy watched as two of the four men rose up and fired several shots at Josie. Awe gripped her when she saw Josie wave her hands in front of her. An intense shield of flames appeared. It was so hot, that the moment the bullets hit it, they dissolved.

"Come on, Josie," Sammy muttered under her breath. "You know you can't keep using that kind of energy for long."

Sammy didn't add that she wished that Dust was here. The men had arrived almost a half hour before.

Josie had told her to take Todd into the house and stay there. Josie had said she was the best one to deal with the men since Dust wasn't there. Sammy and Todd had watched as the four large trucks pulled up. Two men had gotten out of the first two trucks, while the other two stayed in their vehicles.

"Well, well, well, looks like we found something worth keeping, Everett," one of the men said, grinning when he saw Josie standing on the porch.

Sammy couldn't see Josie's face, but she could imagine what the other girl's expression was. The men sounded far too much like Josie's dad and the others back at the silo for her to just dismiss them. She grimaced when she heard the biting sting in Josie's voice.

Yep, Josie wasn't going to be nice, Sammy thought.

"You want to keep something? I suggest you get back in your trucks and keep going," Josie snapped. "There's nothing here for you."

"I think there is," the man named Everett had replied. "We're looking for food and gas."

Josie had tossed her red hair over her shoulder and shrugged. "You and every other survivor on the planet. I said there's nothing here for you; no food, no fuel. Now, move out before I change my mind and decide to see if you have anything that *we* can use instead."

"We...," Everett repeated and raised his hand, motioning for the other two men to get out of their trucks. "How many of you are there?"

Sammy heard Josie's low curse at her mistake. "Stay back," Josie snarled, gripping her hands at her side.

Of course, the men hadn't stayed back; well, at least not until Josie sent the first fire bomb at them. Then, they had all taken refuge behind their vehicles. Sammy heard the shouts of anger and fear seconds before the first sound of a gunshot echoed through the air.

Frightened for Josie, Sammy had been about to release her first arrow when Josie took matters into her own hands. The loud explosion of the truck had shattered the glass in the front rooms and knocked her and Todd onto their backs. When she had looked out again, Josie's body was a glowing mass of flames.

"Kill the witch," Everett yelled, firing at Josie.

Sammy pulled the arrow back and focused. She released it, watching as it soared through the air. Not waiting, she quickly pulled another one and strung it. The loud cry told her that her first arrow had hit its mark.

"Josie, get in the house now," Sammy shouted.

Josie continued to weave her hands in front of her as she stepped back toward the front door. Sammy released another arrow before falling to the floor as the wave of bullets shifted in her direction. Covering her head, she winced as several pieces of glass and wood fragments rained down over her.

She glanced through the doorway when she heard the door slam. Josie lay on the floor, breathing heavily. She was very pale and there were several damp places on her clothing that told Sammy that not all the bullets had missed their mark.

"How bad?" Sammy forced out above the sound of gunfire.

"Just scratches," Josie muttered, wincing as she rolled over onto her stomach. "I could really use a barrel of marshmallows or a case of soda right about now."

Sammy shook her head, turning it when she heard a hoarse cry and the sound of the guns growing silent. Her lips parted and she looked back at Josie with a glimmer of hope. Pushing up, she scrambled back to the window.

"Dust," Sammy breathed, her eyes wide.

Three out of the four men were pressed up against the side of one of the large trucks, their weapons forgotten on the ground. The man named Everett was the only one who wasn't cowering. He couldn't, because he wasn't on the ground, he was several feet above it, held firmly in Dust's grasp.

"Holy shit," Josie whispered next to her. "When did Dust get wings?"

"I don't know," Sammy muttered, her eyes glued to the long, black wings protruding from Dust's back.

Chapter 19

Evolving:

Fury gripped Dust. The hand he held round the man's throat squeezed tighter, causing the man to briefly claw at his wrist. Drawing in a deep breath, he released the man and watched as he crumbled to the ground.

"Get out of here," Dust ordered, the red haze still tinting his vision. "Now! If I see any of you again, I won't give you another chance."

"What… What are you?" Everett demanded in a husky voice, holding his bruised throat as he rose shakily to his feet. "You and that… that bi… girl. What happened to you?"

Dust folded the wings behind him and dropped the few feet to the ground. He glared at the men. When he heard the explosive repetition of gunfire, something strange had washed over him. He remembered vaguely wishing for a moment that he had wings so he could fly over the uneven ground. The next thing he knew, there had been a cloud of sand rising up from the ground around him and he was actually flying! Instead of questioning what was going on, he just accepted it and took advantage to sweep down and snatch the man who was yelling up off the ground.

"It doesn't matter what we are," Dust replied, staring back at the man. "Just leave us alone."

"Everett, Bucky needs help," another man said, kneeling next to the man with an arrow in his shoulder.

Everett glanced over to the pale face of the man that sat next to one of the trucks. He looked back at Dust's hard face. Dust saw Everett's gaze move over the wings on his back. He glared back at the man in warning.

"Get him in the truck. You can take the arrow out once we get on the road," Everett ordered.

"But, he can't drive like this," the man argued, looking back at Dust.

"Then, his truck stays here," Everett snapped, turning away. "Or yours."

"Shit," the man groaned, glancing down at Bucky. "Sorry, Bucky."

"I don't care," Bucky groaned, leaning his head back. "Just get me the hell out of here."

Dust stepped back and watched as the four men piled into two of the trucks. He wanted to turn and run to the house, but he knew that he had to make sure that the men really did leave. The minutes passed in slow, agonizing ticks before he felt confident that the men really were gone and that they weren't coming back. It wasn't until the dust trail settled and he lost sight of the trucks heading south that he turned toward the house.

He had only taken a couple of steps when the door opened and Josie, Sammy, and Todd stepped out onto the battered porch. His gaze flickered over Josie, lingering on the bloodstained sections of her shirt with a dark scowl.

"I'm already healed," Josie said with a grin, holding up a can of soda. "We're out of soda, though.

Dust nodded and looked at Sammy. She was staring at the wings on his back. A crooked grin curved his lips when he saw Todd's mouth hanging open.

"When did you get wings?" Todd asked in awe.

Dust laughed and shook his head. He focused on the dark gray feathers. The feathers dissolved into a pile of sand at his feet.

"I didn't really," he said with a grin.

"Wow!" Todd whispered with a grin and ran down the steps toward him.

Sammy came down the steps, more slowly. She looked at him with a slightly wary expression. Dust frowned, realizing he didn't like her looking at him like that. It reminded him of the first day they met and she saw his chest heal too quickly.

"How did you do that? They looked real," she asked, staring at the pile of sand.

Dust reached out and gently touch her cheek. He waited until she looked him in the eye before he spoke. His thumb rubbed against her skin. It took a moment for him to realize that his hand was shaking a little.

"I'm not sure. It is like I just wished it and it happened. When I heard all the gunshots, I was terrified. I remember wishing I could fly across the ground. The next thing I knew, I was."

Josie walked toward him with a frown. "Can you do it again? Only this time think of something different?" She asked curiously.

Dust shrugged. "I don't know," he admitted.

Josie released an exasperated sigh. "Duh, how about trying?" She suggested with a wave of the soda can in her hand. "I swear, you get to do all the coolest stuff."

Todd glanced at Josie. "I think you can do really cool stuff, too, Josie. You're really good at roasting marshmallows," he said.

Josie rolled her eyes and laughed. "Josie, the marshmallow roaster. Thanks, kid. I'm sure that will be really great on my headstone one of these days," she replied dryly. "Try thinking of something and see if you can do it again."

Dust glanced at Sammy again. He gave her a weak smile before taking a step back. Drawing in a deep breath, he focused on trying to make the wings reappear. A frown creased his brow when nothing happened. Shaking his head, he stared at the pile of sand and focused even harder. Still, nothing happened. After several minutes, he finally looked at the others and shrugged.

"Nothing," he murmured in a puzzled voice. "I don't know what's going on. I can't seem to make it work now."

"Maybe it was just a one time fluke," Sammy suggested with a tentative smile.

"Maybe you need a little motivation," Josie retorted with a devilish gleam in her eye.

"Motivation? Like what?" Dust asked with a puzzled frown.

"Like this," Josie said, throwing up a wall of flames around him and Sammy. "See if you can protect your little girlfriend from getting burned."

Dust started and glared at Josie when she raised an eyebrow at him. He glanced at the circle of fire, it was intensely hot. He reached out and grabbed Sammy, pulling her closer when the ring of fire suddenly started to shrink.

"Josie, knock it off!" Dust snapped.

Josie tapped her chin with her finger, as if thinking, before she shook her head. "I don't think so, Dust. You need to learn if you have a new power," she replied with a sigh, pinching her fingers together with a sly grin. "You should be thanking me. She doesn't seem to mind that you are holding her close now."

"Knock it off, Josie," Dust warned, feeling the anger starting to burn inside him again. "This isn't funny."

"Josie, stop!" Sammy pleaded, turning in Dust's arms to stare at the other girl.

Josie's eyes narrowed and she stared back at Sammy. "Sorry, Sammy. A girl's gotta do, what a girl's gotta do," she replied with a fake, apologetic smile.

"Josie, you aren't really going to hurt them, are you?" Todd asked, staring back and forth with wide eyes.

Dust wasn't so sure. There was a nasty look in Josie's eyes when she stared back at him. The heat of the flames was beginning to become painful. His lips tightened when Josie stared back at him with a combination of defiance and determination. He knew she wasn't going to stop. The red flames in her eyes were almost as hot as the flames licking at the edges of their clothes.

"Dust," Sammy cried out when a section jumped out and caught her pant leg on fire.

Sammy's cry of pain hit Dust hard. He immediately knelt down and patted the fire out. Sammy's hiss told him that the skin underneath had been burned. Anger burst through him and he glared at Josie even as he wished there was some way he could build a wall around Sammy to protect her from the fire.

Almost immediately, the sand around him began to swirl, forming a thin, but impenetrable wall between them and the fire that rose up like a wave. The red-hot flames beat at the protective wall, but couldn't get through it. With a wave of his hand, the sand rose like an ocean wave and fell about the circle of fire, dousing it.

Once the flames were extinguished, Dust flew at Josie, grabbing her by the arms and pushing her backwards against the porch railing. He shook with anger. Twice today, he felt like he was losing control and he didn't like it. It was as if he suddenly didn't have any control over his emotions.

"Well, now we know how to make your new powers work," Josie whispered, staring into his furious eyes.

"Don't, Josie," Dust began, shaking as he held her. "Don't ever threaten her again like that. I'm not sure I can stop from hurting you if you do."

Dust knew he was breathing heavy. His heart was pounding and he was actually shaking with the force of the emotions churning inside him. Something was happening to him. Something more than just the aches and pains he'd had a few days ago. Something more than his being able to control the dirt around him. When it came to Sammy, there was an overwhelming need to protect her from danger that shook and confused him.

"I wouldn't have really hurt her," Josie muttered, glancing over Dust's shoulder at Sammy. "Not on purpose. I was just trying to help you figure out how to use your new powers."

Dust released Josie and stepped back. He shook his head at her. Slowing his breathing, he forced down the confusing feelings coursing through him.

"Just... Don't ever do that again," he warned, turning back toward Sammy.

He stared at Sammy with a look of confusion. She was holding Todd who had rushed to her when he grabbed Josie. A flush of embarrassment swept over his cheeks.

"Get as much stuff together as you can," he said in a quiet voice. "I'll check the truck and see if it has gas in it. If it does, we'll take it. I found more gas and some food. I left it on the side of the road. We'll stop and pick it up. I don't think it is safe to stay here."

"Okay," Sammy replied in a soft voice.

Dust nodded, stepped around her and headed for the truck that was left behind. He kept his head down. If she didn't know that he was interested in her before, she did now. He had a feeling that the look in her eyes would haunt him for a while.

With a sigh, he opened the door to the truck and peered inside. A look of distaste flashed across his face at the garbage piled in the seat and floorboard. He would clean it up after he checked the fluids. He popped the hood and grabbed a pile of napkins on the seat. First things first… Make sure the truck was in good shape, then worry about how he was going to deal with his growing feelings toward Sammy.

..*

Thirty miles south of the farm a dark shape soared above the three trucks moving down the highway. Even from this distance, the hellhound could smell the faint taint of blood. Her mouth watered even as her gaze narrowed on the last truck. She swooped down, following the line of vehicles. The thought that she should wait flashed through her mind before she pushed it away.

No, she thought as she glided in to land on the fabric roof of the last vehicle. *I will feast right under their noses.*

With a quick slice of her front claw, she folded her wings and slipped into the dim interior. On a thick mattress lay a male. A hint of disappointment ran through her. It was not the male she wanted. Still, the smell of fresh blood was thick and made her stomach rumble with hunger.

Creeping forward, she leaned over him. A smile curved her long jaw, revealing sharp teeth. Her long, curved fingers curled around his neck as she leaned down over him and sniffed.

"You… Will… Taste… Good," she forced out in a rough, unfamiliar voice.

The man woke with a start. He started to scream, but she cut the sound with a powerful squeeze to his throat. She "tsked" when she heard a gurgling. The man's eyes bulged in terror and horror, drawing a soft chuckle from her.

"Yes… Human," she whispered. "Fear… Me."

Opening her mouth, she sank her teeth into the soft flesh of his throat and ripped it open. Her hunger driving her to a savagery that splattered blood over the interior of the canvas. Only when she was full did she pull back and lick her lips. Her gaze moved to the thin strip where daylight could be seen. The vehicle was slowing down. Deciding it was time to depart – for the moment – she sliced through the back of the canvas and took off. She landed in a thick clump of trees a short distance away. She would sleep until dark.

I will be hungry again by then, she decided, thinking that fear made the meal so much sweeter.

Chapter 20

Understanding Dawns:

Dust glanced in the rear view mirror for the hundredth time. Sammy and Todd were sleeping in the back seat of the quad cab Toyota Tundra. It wasn't a bad truck after he cleaned all the trash out of it and let it air out a bit.

There was more room in it than he thought there would be. While it wouldn't get as good of gas mileage as the car, it was higher and more powerful. The back of it had a hard top cover so they could put what few supplies they had left in it.

They had stopped and picked up the other supplies from the cart that he had found as well. It was better having the truck for hauling the extra gas, too. They were heading more west than north now. They had tried to head due north, but a missing bridge had forced them to make a detour.

"What is it with you and Sammy?" Josie asked in a quiet voice, turning her head to stare at him.

"Nothing," Dust replied in a clipped tone.

He was still angry at Josie for the little stunt she had pulled earlier. It had flared up again when he caught a glimpse of white bandaging through the burn hole in Sammy's pant leg. His fingers tightened on the steering wheel at the memory.

"Yeah, right. You just wanted to kill all those men and me because you felt 'nothing," Josie replied sarcastically, using her fingers to emphasize the word nothing.

"You hurt her, Josie," Dust retort in a soft voice. "You scared her."

Josie snorted and turned to look out the passenger side window. "I was trying to help. If you've got new powers, we need to know what they are," she muttered.

"Not that way," Dust finally replied. "I meant what I said, Josie. Don't ever threaten Sammy or Todd again. I… I'm not sure I could stop myself from hurting you next time."

"What happened to you?" Josie asked in a quiet voice, turning her head to stare at him.

Dust pursed his lips together. He didn't know what was going on. What happened earlier had taken him by surprise as much as it had Sammy, Todd, and Josie. He'd been trying to figure it out since before they left the old farm house.

"I don't know," he finally admitted with a shrug.

"It could have been because you were sick," a soft voice from the back seat said.

Dust's gaze jerked back to the mirror. For a moment, his eyes and Sammy's connected. He turned his attention back to the road when he heard the thump-y-thump of the reflectors when he started to run off of it.

"I didn't think of that," Josie said, turning around in the seat so she could look back at Sammy with a frown. "But… How?"

***

Sammy briefly glanced at Dust again before she looked away. She had woken up a few minutes before. She listened as Dust and Josie talked, surprised by the feeling of warmth that swept through her when Dust warned Josie not to hurt her or Todd.

If she wasn't honest with herself, she'd admit that she was very confused. Yes, she thought Dust was cute and there had been something about his kiss that made her heart beat faster, but she was also just a little bit scared of him and Josie. How could she be attracted to Dust and scared of him at the same time? When Josie asked him what happened, it had been the same thing that had been bothering her. What had happened that could have changed Dust? The only thing she could think of was he had been sick and it had taken longer for him to heal than before.

"I remember in one of my biology classes the teacher was talking about how your body changes when you get an infection. Once you've been sick, your body recognizes it. Maybe whatever happened to you and Dust… Well, maybe the fever that Dust had kicked his body into gear and changed him some more," Sammy reasoned.

"That actually makes a lot of sense," Josie remarked in a thoughtful tone. "I remember hearing the same thing in school. Something about your white blood cells and stuff. There's no telling what happened to our blood during the fallout. Whatever Dust had might have kicked it into high gear. What did it feel like when you pulled all that sand together? When you were sick, did you feel like you were changing?"

Sammy watched a grimace cross Dust's face before he stared moodily out the front windshield. A moment later, he pulled over into the remains of a what used to be a roadside rest stop. He pulled to a stop and turned off the truck.

"I didn't feel anything. I just felt a sudden need and it happened, but we saw that doesn't always work. When I was sick, I just felt lousy. I hurt all over, especially my back…." His voice faded and he bowed his head and rested his forehead against the steering wheel.

"What is it?" Sammy asked softly, leaning forward and tentatively touching his shoulder.

Dust lifted his head and glanced over his shoulder at Sammy. She could see a worried frown creasing his brow. He looked confused and… frustrated.

"I felt the pain, but it was like it wasn't mine," he admitted in a reluctant voice. "For a little while, it felt like something was trying to rip through my skin, only... It wasn't really my skin."

"That makes absolutely no sense," Josie replied. "How can you feel pain, but it wasn't your pain? Whose pain was it, then?"

Dust scowled and stared out into the growing dusk. Sammy blinked in surprise when he suddenly vanished. One second he was there, the next second he was gone. He reappeared several feet in front of the truck. His shoulders were hunched and his hands were buried in the front pockets of his jeans.

"Stay here," Sammy ordered, releasing her seatbelt and pushing the back door open.

Josie looked at Sammy with wide, startled eyes. "Since when did you get so bossy?" She muttered, but didn't try to get out of the truck.

Sammy ignored Josie's comment and shut the door behind her. She pulled the jacket she was wearing closer around her. The air was definitely chillier. Sliding her hands into the pockets of her jacket, she walked quietly over to where Dust was standing. A light breeze blew his hair, making it even more disheveled than normal. A small, affectionate smile pulled at her lips.

Without thinking about it, she slid her hand out of her jacket and threaded it through his arm. They stood close to each other, not saying anything out loud, but it seemed as if they had an entire conversation in those few minutes of solitude. Sammy released a sigh when Dust's arm moved around her waist and he drew her closer when he felt her shiver.

"I'm sorry," she whispered, leaning her head against his shoulder.

His arm tightened for a moment before he turned her so that she was pressed against him. A shudder ran through his body, something that she felt sure had nothing to do with the cold. She wrapped her arms around him and held him tightly against her.

"You don't ever have to tell me that you're sorry," he murmured.

Sammy leaned back far enough to look up at him. She gave him a weak, uncertain smile that faded as she stared into his eyes. Even though she was several months older than him, he was still taller than she was by almost an inch.

"Yes, I do," she whispered, staring intently at a him. "Ever since Todd and I met you, you've done nothing but protected us. You've put yourself in danger over and over. It is stupid of me to be afraid of you. I know you won't hurt me or Todd."

Dust released a deep breath and glanced out over the barren landscape. She could see the hurt that flashed through his eyes in the growing twilight. Sliding her hand up, she touched his cheek. He turned his head and pressed a kiss into her palm. A small, mischievous grin curved his lips at her startled gasp.

"You're right, you were stupid if you thought I would ever hurt you or Todd." The smile on his lips died and he looked young and confused again. "I don't understand what is going on, but I just know that when I'm with you…." His voiced faded.

"When you are with me…," Sammy encouraged.

Dust looked at her again, his lips tightened into a straight line and he glanced over her head back at the truck. Sammy could feel him pulling away from her. She didn't understand how or why, but she could physically feel him withdrawing from her.

"I need to go for a walk," he muttered. "I'll be back in half an hour. You, Josie, and Todd stay in the truck. Tell Josie… Tell Josie that she better not let anything happen to you. I'll be within hollering distance if you need anything."

"Dust," Sammy started to say before her throat tightened when he dissolved in her arms. "Be safe," she finished with a shake of her head.

Turning, she walked slowly back to the truck and climbed into the driver's seat. She would drive the next section of their journey. Her gaze moved to Todd when he sat up and rubbed his eyes.

"Sammy, I'm hungry," Todd murmured.

"There's some peanut butter and crackers in the bag and a bottle of water," she replied.

"I'm getting tired of peanut butter and crackers," he grumbled. "I want something hot. I wish mom was still alive. I miss her fried chicken and macaroni and cheese."

Sammy's throat tightened and tears burned her eyes. She started when Josie reached down into a bag by her feet and pulled out a can of Beanie Weenies. Her mouth dropped open when Josie popped the top, then rubbed her fingers together until a light blue flame appeared. She held it under the can for a few minutes before wrapping a paper towel around it and handing it to Todd.

"Here you go, kid," Josie said with a wink, pulling a plastic spoon out of the bag as well. "One hot dinner. It might not be fried chicken and Mac and Cheese, but that's about the extent of my cooking abilities."

"Thank you, Josie!" Todd replied with glee. "This is good!"

"Thank you," Sammy whispered, watching as her little brother devoured his hot meal.

Josie shrugged and turned to look back out at the darkness. "I owed you," she muttered. "I… Aw, hell. I'm sorry for what I did earlier. I shouldn't have done that. It was a pretty stupid thing to do."

Sammy reached over and touched Josie's arm, waiting for the other girl to look at her. She couldn't imagine going through everything that Josie had gone through over the last six months or so, especially from her own family. She swallowed when a new thought suddenly hit her hard. They were family now. None of them had anyone else.

"It's okay. I understand why you did it," Sammy was saying when the back door suddenly opened and Dust slid into the truck. His face was pale and an almost desperate look glazed his eyes. "What's wrong?"

"We've got to go," he said in a slightly dazed voice. "Now! We've got to go as far as we can."

"Why?" Josie demanded, turning in her seat even as Sammy started the truck and turned on the lights. "What happened?"

"I know why I felt the burning in my back," Dust said, glancing at Todd before turning his attention back to Sammy and Josie. "I know whose pain I was feeling."

Josie frowned. Sammy glanced at Dust in the mirror. His face was still pale, but there was a new hardness to it that she hadn't seen before. It was as if he had suddenly grown years older in the short time he was gone.

"What's going on, Dust? We need to know if we are going to fight it," Sammy said, pulling out onto the highway and pressing down on the accelerator.

"You can't fight her," he said, looking out at the darkness.

"Her?" Josie asked in confusion. "What her?"

"The devil dog from the town where I met Sammy and Todd," Dust replied in a voice devoid of emotion. "The same one from the silo."

"What? That's impossible," Josie started to argue before she shook her head. "This is nuts! Why? How? None of this makes any sense."

..*

Dust turned to look at Josie. He hadn't understood what was going on. He'd felt strange earlier. There was a feeling of growing restlessness and impending danger. When Josie had asked him about how he was changing, if he felt anything, it had taken a few minutes for him to realize that he was feeling something, but it wasn't really him – it was *her*, the devil dog, that he was feeling.

Nausea threatened to choke him when he remembered the brief connection he'd had with her a few minutes ago. The creature wasn't aware of his presence. He was fairly sure of that. She had been too involved in what she was doing.

"She's changing," Dust murmured, staring at his reflection in the window. "She's different than she was before."

"What do you mean different?" Sammy asked in a worried voice.

"She – The Devil dog can talk," he said with a shake of his head. "She talked to me, back at the silo. She wants our powers."

"I'll roast her ass if she tries to come near me," Josie growled, turning sideways in her seat.

Dust turned to stare coldly at Josie. "She's more powerful than before. The pain I felt in my back – it was her. She has wings. Her body is changing as well. She stands up on two legs now."

"How do you know?" Sammy asked, peering at Dust over her shoulder for a brief second.

"I saw her," he replied in a soft, distant voice.

"Where? Near the rest area?" Josie demanded.

Dust shook his head. "No," he whispered. "She was feeding. I don't think she knows I can sense her. It is like you said, Josie. That one of our kind can sense another of our kind."

"Yeah, but we usually have to be pretty close together," Josie said with a frown. "How far away was she?"

"Several hundred miles," Dust replied.

"What was she doing?" Todd suddenly asked, looking at the other three. "You said she was feeding. What was she eating?"

Dust grimaced. He didn't want to frighten Todd. Swallowing down the nausea that rose in his throat when he remembered what he had seen, he tried to figure out a way to tell everyone so they could understand just how much danger they were all in.

"Do you remember the men from this morning?" He suddenly asked.

"Yes," all three of them replied instantly.

Dust stared grimly back out the window. "They're dead," he replied in a flat, emotionless voice. "She killed them, and enjoyed doing it."

"But, they were headed in the opposite direction!" Sammy exclaimed. "Surely that means she isn't coming after us."

Dust shook his head. "No, she's coming. They were a test for her. She wanted to see if she could kill them without them knowing," he explained.

"How can you be sure?" Sammy insisted, gripping the steering wheel until her knuckles were white.

"Because she told me she was hunting us before we left the silo. I can feel it, as well," he responded in a suddenly dull voice. "She wants me, but...."

"But…?" Josie pressed.

Dust's gaze locked on Sammy. "She wants to kill Sammy first," he said in a tight voice.

Chapter 21

Backtrack:

Sammy focused on the road ahead of them. Dust's words played in her head like a broken record. She fought against the growing panic inside her. Her gaze moved to Dust who was sitting quietly beside her. Josie had climbed into the back seat where, thankfully, she and Todd had fallen asleep.

"Why?" She asked in a soft voice. "Why does she want to kill me first?"

Dust turned to look at her. "I'm not sure," he admitted. "I think it is because she knows I care about you."

"What about Todd and Josie?" Sammy asked with a frown. "Is she after them as well?"

"No," Dust replied quietly.

Sammy gripped the steering wheel and scowled. "You care about them. I just don't get why I'm on her hit list," she said in frustration.

Dust was silent for several minutes. Sammy glanced at him. He wasn't looking at her again. She could feel he was holding something back, she just didn't know what it was. She was just about to ask him when he started talking again in a barely audible voice.

"She's jealous of you," he finally said.

"Jealous? Of me? But… I don't know how to do anything. I mean, look at me! I can't do the things you or Josie can do. I'm not saying I want that creature to come after you and Josie, but still, why me? Why is she jealous of me?"

"Because she knows I care about you in a different way than I care about Todd or Josie. I don't want to kiss or hold them," Dust murmured.

Sammy felt the heat rise to her cheeks. She had been fighting her growing feelings for Dust as well. They were both too young to be thinking about things like that.

"How old are you?" She suddenly asked.

Dust gave her a crooked grin. "I'll be sixteen in a couple of weeks," he said.

"Oh!" Sammy exclaimed with a frown. "You don't kiss like a fifteen year old," she added in a barely audible voice.

Another long silence filled the air. That was one thing about Dust that she liked most of the time and found frustrating at others – his silence. He wasn't one for idle conversation.

"How old are you?" He suddenly asked.

"I'll be seventeen in four months," she replied.

"Oh," Dust muttered. "You kiss pretty good for a sixteen year old."

An amused grin curved Sammy's lips before it faded. She was almost a year older than him, not that it was all that great of an age gap. Her mind returned to their current situation.

"So, what are we going to do?" She asked, glancing at him.

"Run until I can find a safe place to hide you guys, then...," he paused and drew in a deep breath. "Then, I'll find her."

A shiver ran through Sammy at the quiet determination in his voice. This was a side of Dust she had seen numerous times since she first met him. It was the side that scared her.

"You said she was changing, that she was more powerful. What if she hurts you again? What if she kills you?" Sammy asked, voicing her fears.

"She has to be stopped, Sammy," Dust replied. "One way or another. I've seen what she can do. There is a link between us that I don't understand. I just know that she has started killing and she isn't going to stop."

"Then, we should do it together," Sammy finally said. "We are stronger together."

Dust shook his head. "I'd be too worried that she'd get to you. I can't... Sammy, after what happened at the farm when those men were shooting at you. It drove me crazy. Besides, what about Todd? The creature hasn't figured out the connection between him and you. If she did, think of what could happen."

Sammy felt the blood drain from her face. She would never put her little brother in danger. The thought of what could happen to him terrified her.

"At least have Josie with you," she said. "She can take care of herself. You shouldn't have to face it alone. We'll find a place for me and Todd to hide. I can protect us from most things. We need to find more food for you and Josie."

Dust chuckled. "Like a warehouse full of marshmallows," he retorted with a grin. "That would help."

Sammy laughed as well. "Yeah, that would help," she repeated with a yawn. "I'm getting tired and we are getting low on gas."

"Pull over at the next place and I'll fill the tank. We can wake Josie and let her drive for a while," Dust said. "We both need to get some rest."

"Okay," Sammy replied with another yawn. "Thank you again, Dust."

"For what?" He asked in surprise.

Sammy gave him a small, tentative smile and reached out to squeeze his hand. He really didn't know why she was thanking him. That was another thing that she liked about him, even with all that he could do, he was still down to earth.

"For being you," she said, releasing his hand. "I see a shadow of some buildings up ahead. Should I stop?"

"Yeah, we'll just stop for the night. Josie is sleeping pretty good and we all need our rest. A few hours won't matter," he said. "I'll take a look around and make sure it is safe. Maybe we can find some more food and water."

"In the morning," Sammy replied wearily. "I'm beat."

"In the morning," Dust promised.

***

"I found some more," Todd hollered from inside the small store. "These are strawberry flavored."

"I call dibs!" Josie hooted with glee.

Sammy laughed as Josie took off at a run across the store. There wasn't much left, but they were finding a few items including a few bags of the prized marshmallows. Dust looked up at her and grinned. He held a small shopping basket in one hand and a can of some kind of vegetable in the other.

"It looks like someone has gone through the place," he said with a nod at the barren shelves that were still standing. "Fortunately, they missed a few things."

"Including the marshmallow aisle," Sammy replied with a laugh. "You might have a fight on your hands with Josie. Todd has found different flavored ones."

Dust reached in the basket he was holding and lifted out a box of hot chocolate mix – with a big "Marshmallow Lovers" printed on the outside. Sammy rolled her eyes at him. Josie and Dust had been teasing each other all morning about how they were going to have a barter war over who got what. Sammy didn't take it seriously, mostly due to the fact that they included her and Todd in it.

"I want another hot meal," Todd insisted. "Three strawberry marshmallows for it."

"Four and I'll throw in a hot dessert of apple pie filling for you," Josie teased.

Todd frowned for a minute like he was seriously thinking about what she was saying. His face finally cleared and he grinned and nodded. It warmed Sammy's heart to see the laughter in his eyes.

"I'm going to go see what else I can find," Todd said. "Maybe there are some more of those beanie weenies."

"I'll help you," Josie laughed, handing their goodies to Sammy. "Don't let Dust get my marshmallows."

"I won't," Sammy replied dryly.

"How much do we have?" Dust asked, placing the items he had down on the conveyor belt.

Sammy glanced over their treasure trove. It was small, but at least it wasn't all junk food. Still, she would kill for some soft bread and some lunch meat.

"Probably enough for a few days," she said. "Added to what we have, there is about a week's worth of food if we watch what we eat."

Dust nodded. "I want to take another look around and see if I can find some more gas," he said.

"I noticed that the road was partially blocked further down. We'll have to clear it if we want to make it through town," Sammy added with a worried frown. "I wonder what happened to the people that were here. Surely not everyone was killed. It looks like there had been others going through the buildings considering the lack of supplies here."

"I agree," Dust said with a shrug. "I'll see if I can find anything. You and Todd stay close to Josie until I get back."

A flash of irritation swept through Sammy. "You know, we were perfectly fine for over a year before we found you. I think I can watch out for Todd and me," she muttered, looking away from him.

Dust stopped suddenly, turned back around and gripped her arms, pulling her close to him. The strange glitter was back in his eyes again. They glowed with a dark intensity as he stared down into her eyes.

"But you aren't alone anymore," he said.

Sammy's eyes widened when he quickly bent and pressed a hard, possessive kiss to her lips before releasing her. She lifted a shaky hand to touch her burning lips and stared at him as he walked away. Shaking her head, she forced her mind back on the task of inventorying their supplies. In the background, she could hear Josie and Todd talking. A slow smile curved her lips at Dust's reaction to her comment.

"No, we aren't alone anymore," she whispered, packing the items into a second box.

..*

Dust raised his face to the gray sky and drew in a deep breath. His whole body buzzed. He didn't understand why he had grabbed Sammy and kissed her that way. When her eyes flashed with irritation and she snapped that she was capable of taking care of herself and Todd, a sense of panic hit him hard.

"Not just panic," he reluctantly muttered to himself. "Something else, too."

He just didn't know what it was. For the first time in months, he wished his dad was still alive. He could really use another guy to talk to about what was going on and help him understand why he felt the way he did toward Sammy. He sure as heck couldn't ask Josie. She'd have a field day picking on him and Todd was too young.

With a sigh of exasperation, he kicked at a rock in the road. The town was small, just a narrow, two-lane road running through the center with a dozen buildings on each side. There were the remains of houses off the side streets, but almost all of them were in ruins. He seriously doubted that he'd find much in the debris.

He stepped over some fallen bricks, noticing for the first time what Sammy had mentioned back at the store. There was debris from one of the buildings and several abandoned cars blocking the main road. It was possible they might be able to find a way around it, but there was no guarantee. The best bet would probably be to just move the cars and bricks.

Dust stepped closer, noticing where two vehicles were pushed together. He stepped around the side and opened the driver's door. A soft curse escaped him when an arm fell out; or at least the remains of an arm. A pistol fell to the ground at his feet.

"Aw, shoot," he groaned in disgust. "Not more dead bodies."

Swallowing down the nausea that rose in his throat, he stared at the figure slumped in the front seat. The traces of dried blood on the man's bony temple told him that the gunshot had been self-inflicted. Dust glanced at the car in front of him. He wondered if there was someone in that one too. He glanced back toward the store to make sure that Sammy, Todd, and Josie couldn't see the dead guy from the windows.

He took a step toward the other vehicle and peered inside. It was empty. He turned when he heard a sound behind him. His gaze swept over the sign above the building: First Union Bank of Main Street. His eyes narrowed when he saw a movement in the shadows through the open doorway.

Fading, Dust moved through the doorway. He glanced around, tilting his head and listening. There was a muffled sound coming from the back. He walked through the front desk and down the short hallway. He came around just in time to see the door to the vault start to close. He stood indecisive for a moment, trying to decide if he should reform or stay in his present fazed form. Deciding to remain invisible, he strode down the hallway and paused outside of the vault.

"Hurry," a soft voice muttered urgently.

"They are still there," a man's voice said.

"They won't last long," the woman replied. "Just shut the door until they are gone."

Dust bit his lip before he decided he better reform. Turning, he retreated back to the front desk. Maybe whoever was here would be better than Beau and the others back at the silo.

"Hello?" He called out. "I know you're here. I saw you."

"Go away!" A man's voice yelled after a moment of silence.

"Uh, okay," Dust replied.

He waited. From the back, he could hear the frantic whispers between at least two people. When the voices faded, he shrugged. He had enough to worry about at the moment.

"I'm leaving," he called out one last time. "Goodbye. Oh, there is a dead guy in the car out front."

He started to turn when he caught the shadow of a man stepping out from behind the corner leading to the vault. The man held a gun in his shaking hands. Dust grimaced when he saw it pointed firmly at his chest. Raising his hands, he kept them visible above the cashier's desk.

"Who are you?" The man demanded.

"Dust," Dust replied. "Who are you?"

The man stopped and stared at Dust. "I'm Raymond Atwell. I'm the president of the bank," Raymond replied.

"Oh," Dust responded. "Who else is here?"

"Why?" Raymond asked suspiciously.

Dust blinked. "I don't know," he admitted. "I heard other voices. I was just curious."

"Who else is with you?" Raymond Atwell demanded, waving the gun in his hand back and forth.

Dust looked warily at the gun. "If I tell you, will you quit pointing that gun at me?" He asked with a nod of his head.

"Lower the gun, Raymond," a woman ordered. "He's just a boy."

"How do you know that?" Raymond demanded, glancing at the older woman.

The woman huffed and stepped around the man. She stared at Dust with a hard expression before her gaze softened. He gave her a small, crooked smile.

"Ma'am," he replied with a nod of his head.

"How many are with you, boy?" She asked.

"There are three more besides me, ma'am," Dust replied politely.

The woman raised her hand and settled it on top of the gun Raymond was holding, forcing him to lower it. Dust breathed a sigh of relief not to have it pointing at him. He stared curiously at the two people.

"I'm Martha Brookstone," the old woman replied. "I was head cashier of the bank."

"Oh," Dust replied, moving from one foot to the other. "Is there anyone else? We haven't met too many survivors."

"There were close to a dozen of us that survived the initial blast," Martha replied with a sigh of regret. "There are three of us left now."

Dust stared uneasily back and forth. "What happened to the others?" He asked.

Martha shook her head and glanced out the open door. Dust turned to glance in the direction she was staring. He grimaced when he saw the body still visible through the open door.

"Stanley left yesterday evening," Martha replied. "As you can tell, he didn't get very far."

"Yesterday!" Dust repeated in shock, turning to look at the skeletal body again. "But… He's a skeleton."

"It didn't take the bugs long to clean him to the bone," Raymond muttered. "Come dusk, anything outside will end up the same way."

Dust opened his mouth to ask why when a loud scream filled the air. His eyes widened when he recognized Sammy's voice. He turned and darted through the doorway. He ran across the road and down the two store fronts to the grocery store. He saw Sammy coming out from between two buildings.

He grabbed her and pulled her into his arms. She was shaking so badly, he was amazed that she could stand. His gaze darted to Josie and Todd as they pushed through the doorway.

"What is it?" Josie demanded, her fists clenched and her eyes glancing wildly around.

"I don't know," Dust said. He pulled back and brushed Sammy's hair back from her face. "What is it?"

"Skeletons," Sammy choked out, staring up at Dust in terror. "Hundreds of skeletons."

"Stay here," he ordered, glancing at where Raymond, Martha, and another young girl stood outside the bank.

He reluctantly released Sammy and stepped around her. Walking over to the narrow cut between two buildings, he walked down the long alley. He stopped at the end and covered his nose with his arm.

Sammy was right. Hundreds of corpses, some human, but most of them from various animals, lay piled up in a large mound. Most were stripped of all their flesh. A few were still partially covered. He staggered backwards several steps before he turned. The world was becoming more and more bizarre. Striding back down the alley, he broke back out onto the street. His gaze locked with Raymond Wellington.

"What happens at dusk?" Dust demanded, striding toward the small group.

"The bugs come out at night," Martha whispered. "We are running out of food. They don't want regular food. They want us. We've tried to leave, but no one ever makes it out."

"Why don't you leave before it gets dark?" Sammy asked in a shaken voice. "We need to leave right now."

"They ate through all the wires on the cars," Raymond replied. "Stanley worked on trying to get this one started. They must have been in the seats or something. They swarmed him the minute he started it. They are attracted to the electrical system."

"We've been hiding in the vault every night," Martha replied. "It is the only place safe from them.

The first night they killed half of us. Six of us made it to the bank and hid in the vault."

"But people kept trying to leave," Raymond replied. "Denise, Martha and I are the last. Denise hasn't spoken since that first night."

"What are we waiting for? We need to get out of here, then," Josie said with a look of disgust. "I sure as hell don't want to end up getting eaten alive."

Dust glanced at Josie and nodded. "Sammy, I want you, Todd, and the others to get what food we've collected and put it in the truck. We'll squeeze into," he ordered. "Josie, I want you to come with me. Bring a bag of the marshmallows, we're going to need it."

Josie's eyebrow rose, but she didn't argue. Instead, she disappeared into the store before returning a moment later with a bag of the strawberry marshmallows. Dust nodded to Sammy when she looked at him with a pleading look in her eyes. He could feel her terror.

"We'll be back in a few minutes. Be prepared to leave," Dust replied.

"We will," Sammy whispered. "Come on, Todd. Let's get the food."

"What are you going to do?" Raymond asked, stepping forward.

Dust paused, glancing at Josie, before turning his attention to the man. "They deserve a proper burial, or at least not to be left that way. Just help Sammy and Todd. It won't take us long," he promised.

Raymond paled, but nodded. "Are you sure we can get out of here?" He asked in a hesitant voice.

"Yes, if we hurry. We'll have to back track to the south some," Dust replied, turning away. "We've just got to hurry.

Dust didn't wait. It was already early afternoon and the skies were beginning to grow dark with storm clouds. He didn't want to take a chance on the bugs coming out. He also hated that they would be heading back the way they came. That meant they would be heading in the same direction as the She Devil that was after them.

"Holy crap," Josie whispered and blanched when she saw the pile of bones.

"I'm going to open the ground up. I want you to burn them," Dust ordered, taking the bag of marshmallows and opening it. "Make it hot, Josie."

Josie swallowed and nodded. She reached into the bag and started stuffing the pink sugary confection into her mouth, all joy gone from the surge of power rushing through her. She didn't question how he was going to open up the ground. Dust wasn't sure if he could do it, he just knew it needed to be done.

Focusing, he bent down and touched the ground. He imagined a hole forming around the huge pile of remains. The ground trembled and groaned before a large hole suddenly opened up under the thick mass.

"Now, Josie," Dust ordered through clenched teeth. "Make it hot!"

Dust watched the mass. Something told him that Josie needed to hurry. Her hands were waving back and forth. At the same time as the flames shot out, a mass of black rose up through the skeletons. The bugs were sleeping under the mass.

"Hotter, Josie! Don't let them out," Dust yelled above the high pitch sound of the insects struggling to climb out of the expanding hole. "Hotter!"

Josie's body glowed with the heat of the flames she was pouring down into the hole. The loud screeching and popping of cooking insects was sickening, but she didn't waver from her gruesome task. Dust kept his eyes on the hole, making sure that none of the insects escaped. Every time they tried, he would deepen the hole. Only when nothing but ash remained did he stand up, bringing a wave of dirt up and over the hollowed out tomb. It fell like rain, covering the fine ash that remained.

Josie's hands fell to her sides and she swayed. "I need a soda," she whispered, staring palely down at the gradually filling hole. "That has to be the most disgusting thing I've ever had to do."

Dust didn't respond. He just focused on filling every inch of the hole until there was no evidence of the horrors that lay beneath the soil. Only when the last bit fell did he whisper a few words for the victims. He suddenly felt older than his fifteen years.

"Let's go," he finally said, turning and wrapping his arm around Josie when she swayed again.

With a sigh, he bent and lifted Josie into his arms. She clung weakly to him. He would make sure she had one of those sodas when they got back to the truck.

"You did good, Josie," he murmured quietly as he carried her down the alley. "You did real good."

She turned and buried her face in his neck. "Just don't ask me to do that again," she ordered in a thick voice.

"I'll try not to," Dust said, feeling Josie's damp, hot tears against his skin.

A short time later, they were heading out of town, going back the same way they had traveled the night before. They would need to find another way around. Raymond, Martha, and Denise sat in the back while he, Sammy, Todd, and Josie squeezed into the front seat. It wasn't easy. Sammy refused to let Todd ride without his seatbelt, so she sat on the center console, while Todd and Josie squeezed into the passenger seat.

"We'll have to find a different vehicle, or another one that is big enough for all of us," Dust said quietly.

"When we can," Sammy replied in a somber voice. "I just want to get away from that place."

Chapter 22

Shelter, Dreams and Old Enemies:

Dust rubbed wearily at his eyes. Their escape from the town and subsequent run had worn him out. They had passed through several small towns, but very little remained of them. There had also been a huge storm, which hadn't helped. They had driven as long as they could before the rain became too heavy to see out the windshield. They had finally found the remains of a high school gym.

"It looks okay," Dust said to the small group. "Josie, did you and Sammy find anything?"

"No nasties," Josie replied. "Todd found a snack machine, though. We bagged what we found."

"There's a couple of soda machines in the concession area. We didn't get them opened yet. There was more chips and some really green and black looking hot dog and hamburger buns if you feel like living dangerously. We didn't open the freezer," Sammy added.

"We didn't find anything either," Raymond said.

Dust looked around the dim interior. A faint layer of dirt covered the wood floor. At each end of the court were basketball hoops with a ghostly scoreboard mounted on the wall behind them. The bleachers were extended, as if waiting for a crowd of students to file in.

"Denise and I found some exercise mats in a storage closet. They would make a nice bed," Martha said.

"I checked around outside. I found a generator, but I'm not sure how much good it will do or if it will even work. I didn't see any other cars. The only thing I found was a school bus," Dust said. "It is too dark to see if I can get it started. I think the best thing would be to get some rest and check it out in the morning."

"What if there are more bugs here?" Raymond asked in a hesitant voice. "I think we should take turns keeping watch."

Dust nodded. He ignored the fatigue pulling at him. Raymond was right. They should post a guard.

"I'll take the first watch," Sammy said. "Martha and Denise can take the next one."

"I can help you, Sammy," Todd piped up. "Or Josie."

Josie grinned. "You just want some of my marshmallows," she teased.

Todd giggled. "I like it when you roast them," he laughed.

Dust and Sammy glanced at Todd. They hadn't shared with Raymond, Martha, and Denise the special talents that Dust and Josie possessed. After the way Josie's dad had reacted, they didn't want to take a chance.

"Deal," Josie replied. "I found a deck of cards in one of the desk drawers in the locker room. I'll teach you how to play poker."

"Cool!" Todd exclaimed in excitement. "Can we take first watch, Sammy?"

Sammy laughed and nodded. "If Josie doesn't mind," she said, looking at the other girl. "You'll keep an eye on him?"

Josie rolled her eyes. "Of course," she muttered. "He's my little man, aren't you, Todd?"

"Yep," Todd replied with a grin. "I'm her little man."

"I found a metal barrel outside. Raymond, if you help me bring it in, we can find what we need to build a fire in one of the locker rooms. It might be warmer in there. It feels like another storm is coming," Dust said. "Sammy, can you see what we've got for dinner?"

"Something hot," Todd added with a hopeful look.

"I'll see what we've got," Sammy replied with a soft smile.

"Denise and I will help make up the beds, then help you with dinner," Martha replied with a warm smile. "This is the first time in over a year that we haven't been terrified. I can't thank you enough."

"Me… Either," Denise forced out, tears glittering in her eyes.

Martha's eyes widened and she turned to the young woman and hugged her close. Dust watched for a moment before his gaze locked with Sammy's in a silent sense of satisfaction. Turning away, he listened to Todd as the young boy excitedly told Denise about the Beanie Weenies that Josie had warmed up for him. He was just thankful Todd left out how she had done it.

..*

It was after midnight when Dust woke up. Outside he could hear the sounds of another storm beating against the roof. They had found a delivery area for the gym and had broken the lock so they could pull the truck inside. The bus was parked near the building already and he just hoped it survived.

Worry gnawed at him, keeping him from going back to sleep. They were almost out of gas for the truck. If they didn't find fuel soon, they would be hard pressed to continue on. It was also difficult traveling with seven of them in the small confines of the truck cab. The bus would be nice, but it would get even worse gas mileage than the truck and they would have to find some diesel fuel for it.

He turned his head when he heard soft footsteps. Josie and Todd came into the locker room. He heard Josie softly talking to Sammy. His gaze followed Sammy when she stood up and ran a hand down over her face. She bent and picked up the bow and sheath of arrows that she had retrieved from the truck.

Rolling over, he silently rose to his feet and grabbed his jacket. He knew he should try to get some more rest, but it would have to wait. His mind was running on overtime.

Dust quietly followed Sammy out of the locker room. A shiver escaped him when he stepped into the large gym area. He hadn't realized just how much warmth the fire was putting out.

"What are you doing up?" Sammy asked in surprise. "This is my shift."

Dust shrugged. "I know," he said, thrusting his hands into his front pockets. "It's colder than it was last night."

"I think the whole planet is beginning to cool down," Sammy whispered. "I wonder if we should have headed south instead of north."

"We can head down the coast of California if my aunt and uncle didn't make it," Dust said, walking toward the bleachers. "I guess it is kind of stupid to try to find them."

Sammy followed him. Together they climbed to the top and sat close to where the ceiling connected with a series of small windows that were protected by the overhang of the roof. They sat side by side and looked out at the storm.

"I don't think it is stupid. If we had any relatives, I'd be searching for them, too," Sammy murmured, staring out the window. "What are we going to do if we can't find any gas?"

Dust snorted and shook his head. "I was just thinking the same thing," he said with a short laugh before it faded. "I don't know. We have enough to fill the truck about half full. We'll look at the map and see if there is – were any towns close by. If the weather clears up enough, we can check out this one as well. There must have been a gas station here. If there was, there might be gas left in the underground tanks. We just have to find it."

"What about the devil dog? We lost most of the distance we were putting between us. Have you been able to connect with her again?" Sammy asked in a quiet voice.

Dust looked away from her. He rubbed his hands on his thighs before folding them together to keep them warm. A worried frown creased his brow. He had lost contact with the creature. He wasn't sure if it was because of the weather or the She Devil had realized that he could sense her and was blocking him or if it was because they were too far apart; whatever it was, he couldn't tell where she was at the moment and that worried him.

"No, I haven't been able to," he finally replied.

He started when he felt Sammy's fingers slide over his hands. She pulled his hands apart and held his left hand in hers. She rubbed her thumb across his palm.

"It will be alright," she said in a quiet voice. "There is no sense in worrying about the things we can't change. If she comes, we'll fight. Just like we've done every day since the earth changed."

"Sammy," Dust started to say before he shook his head and looked out of the window. His fingers tightened around her hand. It felt good to touch someone else. It felt good to touch her. He turned his head to look back at her. "I don't know what tomorrow will bring, but I'm glad we found each other."

"Me, too," she said, releasing his hand and rising to her feet. "Go get some sleep. You definitely deserve it. I'll wake Raymond in a few hours."

Dust nodded and rose to his feet. "Be careful. If you hear anything you aren't sure about, wake me," he told her.

Sammy stepped closer and rose up to brush a kiss across his cheek. "You are a really special guy, Dust," she murmured before she bent and picked up her bow and quiver of arrows. "Go get some rest."

Dust watched Sammy walk back down the bleachers. Releasing a sigh, he shoved his hands back into his pockets and slowly stepped down to the gym floor. He returned to the locker room. Everyone was asleep. His lips twitched when he heard Raymond and Todd both snoring.

He added another piece of wood from an old pallet to the barrel before he sank down on the thick foam mat. He pulled his blanket over him, lay back and stared up at the ceiling. It didn't take long for the fatigue of the last few days to sink in. His eyelids felt like someone had placed weights on them and he slowly sank deeper into the dark pit of exhaustion.

..*

Storm clouds swirled around him. Dust turned in a circle, surprised that he didn't feel the icy blast of wind cutting across the barren landscape. He must be in his faded form, he thought vaguely as he gazed across the flat field. Green lightning danced through the sky. Every once in a while, he would see it make a pattern along the ground.

He felt his stomach grumble and reached down to rub it. His hand froze when he felt the taut, full belly. Looking down, a shudder went through him when he saw the black flesh. This wasn't his body. In that moment, he realized he was once again connected with the She Devil.

"I feel you," she whispered.

A shiver ran through Dust. She had changed even more in her physical appearance. Her body was sleek with a fine covering of black hair. Her face had changed as well. She still had the muzzle of a dog, though it was less pronounced than before. What had really changed were her eyes and brow. She reminded him of Anubis, the ancient Egyptian creature that was half dog and half man. The only difference was her long, black leathery wings that were folded around her to keep her warm. She had found refuge in one of the old buildings they had passed a few days ago. She was closer, but they still had several hundred miles between them.

"Why are you hunting me?" Dust demanded.

"Power," she responded. "You have a power that I want."

"What power? You are powerful in your own right. Killing me won't change that," Dust insisted. "You shouldn't kill others."

"Those I kill are weak. They serve no purpose but to feed me," she replied with a shrug.

"You didn't answer my question," Dust pointed out. "Why do you think killing me will give you my powers?"

"I don't want to kill you. I want power that you have," the She Devil responded in a soft voice. "Only one. I will have it. You will give it to me."

"I don't know what you are talking about," Dust argued. "What power?"

"The girl must die," the She Devil whispered instead.

Dust could feel the connection between them beginning to fade. A powerful sense of fear and frustration burned inside him. There was something he was missing; something very, very important that he needed to know, to understand.

"Why? Why, must she die?" He asked, clinging to the faint thread between them.

"You are the new beginning," the She Devil replied in a husky voice filled with longing. "I must be your mate, not her."

Dust woke with a start. Despite the cold, he could feel the clammy sweat beading on his brow. His gut twisted sickeningly at the thought of physically touching the She Devil. She was convinced he had some strange power. He didn't know what she was talking about, but he heard the conviction in her voice. She wanted him and she wanted whatever she thought he had, but most of all, she wanted Sammy dead.

"Never," Dust whispered, turning his head when Raymond suddenly came into the room.

He sat up, staring at the older man. He must have been asleep longer than he thought. There was a slight red haze to his vision. The one he got whenever he thought of Sammy being in danger. He quickly blinked to clear his vision. Raymond's lips were pressed tightly together and his face was twisted into a wary expression.

"What is it?" He asked, pushing the blanket aside.

"We have company coming," Raymond said.

The others stirred, sitting up and blinking sleepily around them. It didn't take long for Raymond's words to sink in. Each of them quickly rose to their feet.

"How many?" He asked. "What about the storm?"

"The storm died down several hours ago," Raymond replied, checking the gun he held. "The sun is just beginning to rise. I saw headlights in the distance. They are getting closer. I thought I should tell you."

Dust nodded and looked at Sammy and Josie. "Raymond and I will see who it is," he said. "You and Josie take up position in case they aren't nice."

"I need a soda or something to eat," Josie muttered, turning to where a box of food was on the table. "You'd better eat something, too."

"Why do you need to eat if someone is coming?" Martha asked in confusion, wrapping her arm around Denise when the girl moved closer to her.

"'Cause they need it for their powers," Todd said without thinking. He flushed when he realized what he had said. "Sorry, Dust. Sorry, Josie."

"What powers?" Raymond asked with a frown.

"You might as well tell them, Dust," Josie muttered, opening a can of soda and taking a long gulp before she wiped a hand across her mouth. "They are bound to find out sooner or later if they are with us."

Dust released an exasperated breath and ran his hand through his disheveled hair. He winced when his fingers caught in it. He needed to see if Sammy or Josie could cut it soon. He looked warily back and forth between Raymond, Martha, and Denise. Josie was right, if they were going to be traveling together, it was only a matter of time before they found out about what he and Josie could do.

"What are we bound to find out about?" Raymond asked, gripping the gun in his hand.

Dust briefly glanced at Josie. She was watching Raymond with an intense stare. She might act like she wasn't paying attention to the way the older man was holding the gun, but he could see the red flames in her eyes.

"After the comet hit the earth, some strange things happened to some of us," Dust replied.

"You mean like the bugs?" Martha asked.

Dust nodded. "Yes, like the bugs and other – creatures – that we have encountered. Josie and I were also affected by whatever it was," he said with a calm that belied his true feelings. "Josie can control fire."

"Control fire…?" Martha whispered in confusion, glancing at Josie.

"Yeah, like this," Josie responded, rubbing her fingers together until tiny blue flames danced from the ends of them. "And, this…."

Dust grimaced when Josie closed her hand for a moment before opening it and tossing a small fireball into the fire barrel. *Leave it to Josie to set the stage on fire,* he thought in exasperation. He glanced at where Martha, Denise, and Raymond had scooted together until they were practically on top of each other.

"What… What can you do?" Raymond asked in a trembling voice.

"Different things," Dust admitted. "What matters is that we won't hurt you. We'll use our talents to help protect you. I promise."

"It's true," Sammy said, stepping closer to Dust. "He has saved Todd and me numerous times since we first met him."

"And Josie can roast marshmallows over her fingers," Todd added. "They are really good."

A nervous giggle escaped Denise. Her gaze moved from Todd to Josie. Her lips were parted in wonder as she stared at the flames.

"Can you do anything, Sammy?" Denise asked in a soft, husky voice.

Sammy shook her head. "Not like them, but I can use this," she said, lifting the bow.

Raymond was silent for several long seconds. Dust heard the slight tremor in the man's voice, but he looked him square in the eye when he finally spoke. There was a hint of respect and awe in the man's gaze that made Dust a touch embarrassed.

"That's how you took care of the remains back in town," Raymond said.

"Yes," Dust replied with a sharp nod.

"I hate to break this up," Josie interrupted. "If we have company coming, I'd just as soon be there when they arrive so I can know if they are friend or foe."

"You're right," Raymond said in a hasty tone. "Martha and I can greet them. Denise, you and Todd stay hidden. Dust, perhaps it would be better if you, Josie, and Sammy covered us. I can shoot a gun, but I'm not as good as I used to be."

"Josie, you take the left side of the building. Sammy, you take the right," Dust instructed, grabbing the soda and draining it before he handed it back to Josie.

"Where will you be?" Raymond asked.

"Behind them," Dust said, fading.

"Shit!" Raymond muttered, stumbling backwards.

"You haven't seen anything yet," Josie promised, stepping around them. "Let's see if there are going to be any fireworks or not."

Dust left the small group. He hurried through the building and out through the front doors. He could see the large truck moving closer. They may just be survivors looking for food and fuel. There was no way that was going to happen if the bus started.

Dust settled on top of the bus and re-materialized. He lay down flat. From the angle the bus was parked, he could see both the front door of the gym and the road leading up to it. Josie came out a moment later and darted to a small pile of dirt that had been dumped to fill in the pot holes. Sammy came out and glanced around before moving to stand near the remains of an old shed. Once the truck stopped, he would move up behind it.

Five minutes later, the truck slowed down before pulling to a stop about twenty feet from the gym. Dust couldn't see through the windshield. It was coated with a thick layer of grime. Only a thin section of streaked glass from the windshield wipers gave the driver and passenger enough space to peer through.

Dust's head turned and he watched as Raymond and Martha cautiously stepped out of the gym. He turned his gaze back to the truck as both doors slowly creaked open. From his position, he could see a dirty boot emerge from the driver's side before the rest of the man's body followed. His jaw hurt and his eyes narrowed when he saw the long rifle in the man's hand. The man's face was shielded from his view by a wide brim hat.

The man slammed the door to the truck and took several steps forward, stopping in front of the re-enforced front grill and bumper. Dread built up in Dust when a second man with a more slender build walked around the side of the truck to stand next to the man.

Sometimes, he thought silently. *Sometimes, I just wish life could be normal for more than a day or two.*

"Hello," Raymond called out in greeting. "Where did you come from?"

"I'll tell you where they both came from," Josie growled, her hair swirling around her in dark rage.

"I'll tell you where I'm going to be sending them back to, as well."

"Hello, Josie," the big man said in a quiet voice, raising his shotgun.

"Hello, daddy," Josie sneered, raising her hands. "I thought you and brother dearest were dog food."

Beau's lips twisted. "We almost were," he admitted.

Dust was surprised when Beau suddenly lowered his shotgun. The old man lifted his hand and removed his hat. One side of his face was ravaged with long, deep scars. His right eye was covered with a patch.

"Ouch, that looks like it might have hurt just a little bit," Josie replied unsympathetically.

"It did," Beau finally said. "I've been looking for you."

"Why?" Josie demanded, clenching her burning fists. "To finish off what you started? I'm not going to let you chain me up and starve me again. I'm sure as hell not going to let you kill me."

Beau carefully reached down and propped his shotgun up against the front of the truck. He murmured softly to Randolph to do the same. It took a moment for Josie's brother to comply.

"I was wrong, Josie," Beau said, stepping away from the truck. "This world… It needs creatures like you in it. We need creatures like you. There's no way normal humans can fight against those beasts and win. It came through a twelve foot thick wall, Josie. Not even the silo is a safe place to be."

"You know Randolph is like me, don't you?" Josie snarled, not moved by her father's confession. "Let him save you."

"Dad knows, now. I'm not as strong as you are, Josie," Randolph muttered.

"It was Randolph who saved my life," Beau added. "He knew when the creatures were coming and from where. It was the only thing that saved us."

"Yeah, well, if you've got him. That still doesn't explain why you're looking for me," Josie replied nastily.

"Do you know if Maria and the kids got out?" Beau asked instead.

"Yes, they did, along with Alex. They aren't with us, though," Dust answered as he reformed slightly behind Beau. He quickly realized that Josie could very well torch her father and brother. While they might deserve it for what they did to her and the others like them, killing them wouldn't change the past and would only leave more scars on Josie. "What do you want, Beau? We haven't forgotten what you did back at the silo or that you held a gun to Todd's head and threatened to kill him. It doesn't make much sense coming here looking for our help after you've threatened all of us like that."

Beau jerked around, his one good eye narrowing on Dust. His lips tightened into a crooked line, the right side of his mouth pulled at the still pink scars of healing tissue. He rubbed a hand down the left side of his face.

"I figured you must have been different," Beau muttered. "Randolph wasn't sure. He sensed something was off with you, but we couldn't tell for sure. He can't read you like he does the others. I shouldn't have threatened the boy, I'll admit that. It was wrong."

Dust didn't reply. There was really nothing to say. Asking for forgiveness didn't go far if you didn't really mean it. Still, if Randolph could sense the She Devil, it might come in handy in preventing any more deaths. Dust glanced over at Randolph who was looking down at the ground.

"Is it true that you can sense where the devil dogs are and when?" Dust asked instead.

Randolph glanced up at him and nodded. "Yeah," he responded in a quiet voice. "Especially…."

Dust frown when Randolph's voice faded and he glanced at his dad. Something was going on. He glanced at Josie. Her whole body was glowing now. In the background, he could see Raymond and Martha staring at Josie in terror and fascination. He finally turned back to Randolph.

"If you want us to trust you, you need to be honest with us," Dust stated in a cold, calm voice.

"Trust! I'd sooner trust that She Devil than those two," Josie growled.

Dust didn't miss Randolph's jerk of surprise or the flush that flared up his cheeks. Beau grunted and turned to glare at Josie. For a moment, Josie and her dad looked so much alike that Dust had to keep the twinge of amusement from showing on his face. Two hardheaded, hot-tempered forces were clashing head-on. Unfortunately, Beau didn't stand a chance against his pissed-off daughter.

"Darn it, girl, I'm trying to tell you I'm sorry," Beau snapped. "You were always too hardheaded for your own good. Randolph thinks the beast that attacked us is coming after you. I should have just left you to deal with it on your own for all the appreciation you are giving us for risking our necks to come save you!"

"Save me!" Josie flared, turning from a vivid orange and red flame to a brilliant blue in her anger. "I could turn you and that damn devil dog to ash with a snap of my fingers."

"Josie," Randolph replied, raising his hands up and stepping in front of their dad. "You're right. I just… I'm sorry. I'm sorry."

Dust didn't miss the way Randolph's eyes shifted from Josie to where Sammy had stepped out from behind the old shed. A dark look of regret flashed through his eyes before he glanced away again. While he didn't like the idea of Randolph and Beau being around, he also knew that if Randolph could sense the She Devil coming, maybe they could use that to their advantage. Dust could sense her, but it was hit or miss.

"Randolph, can the devil dog sense you?" Dust asked, stepping closer.

Randolph turned and looked at him. After a brief second, he shook his head. Dust breathed a sigh of relief.

"No, but I can tell she is headed this way," Randolph said. "She was to the southeast of us. For some reason, I can lock on to her, but I don't think she is aware of it. She knows where you are, though. It wasn't hard to figure out where to go based on that. The only advantage we had was that she seems to stop pretty frequently."

"She has to feed," Dust stated in a grim voice. "Her body is changing too fast for her to keep going."

"We already know she's coming," Josie snapped, stepping closer. "Move aside, Dust. I'll give them to the count of twenty before I start throwing fireballs at them."

Dust turned and grimaced at Josie. "You can't kill them, Josie, no matter how much they deserve it," he informed her with a wave of his hand.

"Why not? I don't see anything stopping me but you," Josie replied. "We can always see if you're fire proof now."

"Knock it off, Josie," Sammy interjected. "We need him, don't we, Dust?"

"Yes," Dust replied.

Josie glared back and forth between Sammy, Dust, and her brother. The flames covering her body flickered before dying and she placed her hands on her hips and violently shook her head back and forth.

"Oh, no. *Really?! Are you kidding me?* After all they have done, you're just going to welcome them with open arms?" Josie demanded in disbelief.

"Josie, we know that creature is coming," Sammy said. "If Randolph can give us even a small advantage, it could be the difference between life or death for some or all of us."

"I... Don't... Care!" Josie replied vehemently. "I'll take my chances."

"You might be willing to take the chance with your life, but I'm not prepared to do that with Todd's," Sammy said in a soft voice. "Once she is dead, they can go their own way. Until then, as much as I hate it too, we need their help."

Josie's jaw worked furiously as she stared at her father and brother. Dust could see the conflict in her expression. She finally threw her hands up in the air and turned sharply on her heel. He watched as she strode angrily back toward the gym.

"If they so much as sneeze in my direction I'm going to roast them," Josie snarled as she pushed past a stunned Raymond and Martha. "I *really* hate my family!" She added in a loud voice before she disappeared back inside.

Dust's lips twisted in amusement. He turned back to look at Beau and Randolph. He could see the disgruntled look on Beau's face.

"She's really not so bad," Dust said.

"Oh yes, she is," Beau grunted. "She's just like I was at that age. That's why we can't stand one another."

Sammy came up to stand next to Dust. "It might also be because you practically starved her to death, chained her, and locked her in a concrete tomb," she pointed out.

"Yeah, well, that might have a little to do with it, as well," Beau muttered, starting to turn away. "I've got weapons. We need to decide how we're going to stop that thing."

Chapter 23

Family:

Dust sighed and looked over at Josie sitting on a pile of pallets. She was staring, moodily, out at the empty road. Ever since her dad and brother arrived, she'd hardly said two words to anyone.

"I was wrong," Beau muttered, holding the end of a thick water hose they had found. They had cut a section of it and were siphoning diesel fuel out of a barrel they had discovered near the remains of a dilapidated old bus shed. "If we'd had her help, we probably could have killed those damn creatures."

Dust looked down at the other end of the hose where it disappeared into the gas tank of the small school bus. With a little work, the bus had started. The tires weren't in the best shape, but at least they weren't rotted. He figured being up against the building helped protect it from the worst of the weather.

"Probably," he finally said when Beau had grown silent again. "It might help if you were to tell her that."

Beau grunted. "She won't believe me," he replied, spitting on the ground.

Dust looked at the ravaged face of the old man. "She might," he said. "Or she might not. Either way, you should tell her."

He saw Beau glance over at Josie again. A reluctant smile curved his lips when Beau muttered a soft curse and straightened. Beau might have been the boss back in the silo, but here, he was just like the rest of them – vulnerable to what the world threw at him.

"Guess it can't hurt none," Beau said with a sigh. "If she sets me on fire, just let me burn. I'll be the first to admit I was never the best father or husband and I probably deserve it."

"Yeah, you're right. You weren't the best dad," Dust agreed.

Beau shot Dust a nasty look out of his good eye. "I did what I thought was right," he snapped.

"Killing people because they are different is never right. That's the only reason I tried to stop the She Devil from killing you," Dust murmured, glancing back at Josie. "Josie's heart is in the right place."

"If you say so," Beau muttered, casting another glance at Josie.

Beau spit again before he released the hose and reached for the rag in his back pocket. Dust could see the look of uncertainty on Beau's face before it hardened into the familiar mask he normally wore. He shook his head and watched Beau walk warily toward Josie.

..*

Josie raised her face to the chilly breeze. She wished it could freeze her heart so that she couldn't feel the pain radiating through her. Of course, if it did, she'd just melt it. Bending, she picked up a rock and rolled it between her fingers.

The sound of footsteps drew her attention back toward the gym. A dark scowl crossed her face when she saw her dad walking toward her. He slowed and stared back at her with a wary expression, his gaze flickering from her face to her hand.

Josie glanced down and grimaced when she saw that the rock in her hand glowed a bright red. Drawing in a deep breath, she focused on the flames until they went out. Her lips pinched in distrust when he kept walking toward her.

"I wouldn't, old man," she warned.

Beau's lips pursed together in irritation. "I want to talk to you," he replied in a sharp tone.

"Well, I seem to remember being very specific about what I would do to you and Randolph if either one of you came near me," she retorted angrily.

"I'm going to say what I've got to say and you are going to listen," Beau snapped in a stubborn tone.

Josie rose from the pallets and clenched her fists by her side. She could feel the power surging in waves inside her. As far as she was concerned, there was no need for any type of discussion.

She and her dad had never gotten along. Nothing had changed. She didn't care if he came looking for her. He'd only did it to save his and Randolph's sorry butts, not because of any feelings of love or concern.

The world was a bigger and badder place than her dad thought he was and he didn't like it. Well, too… damn… bad! It wasn't her monkey. It wasn't her circus! She belonged to a different freak show now – a freak show where she was one of the normal ones. It was also one where she could pick who her family was going to be.

"Stay away from me," Josie muttered and turned to walk away.

"Damn it, girl, I just wanted to tell you I was wrong," Beau growled and ran a stained hand down over the good side of his face before he released a deep, loud breath. "I was wrong."

Josie stood stiffly, looking at him in disgust. "Do you think saying you were wrong is going to make everything better? Do you think I'm supposed to forget that you treated me like some deranged animal?" She asked in disbelief, turning to face him.

Beau's face hardened. "As far as I knew you could have gone crazy and killed everyone! I did what I thought needed to be done. At least, I didn't kill you," he added at the end, his voice fading as he looked away from her.

Josie stared at her dad with growing disbelief. Even now, he was making excuses for what he had done to her and to the others like her that were 'different'. She stared at the ravaged side of his face. Bitterness fought with pity.

"You have always been a judgmental son-of-a-bitch," she whispered with a shake of her head. "I guess mom was the lucky one out of all of us, after all."

Beau turned back to glare at her. "She's dead," he replied with a frown.

"I know," Josie answered in a quiet voice before she turned and walked away.

***

Several hours later, Dust was finishing up on the bus when Josie came around the end. She had her hands in the front pockets of her jeans and her head down. Dust wiped his grimy hands on the towel hanging from the mirror.

"You okay?" He asked, walking toward her. Josie lifted her chin and shrugged. Her gaze didn't quite meet his and her lips twisted with a bitter smile. He came to a stop in front of her and waited. "Hey," he murmured, reaching up to touch her chin.

Josie's eyes filled with tears. She tried to hide them, but failed when one slipped down her cheek. Dust wasn't sure what to do. This was a side of Josie he had never seen before. Reaching out, he pulled her into his arms and just held her.

"I hate my family," Josie whispered in a broken voice.

"Yeah, I would too if they were mine," Dust replied.

A choked giggle escaped Josie and she shook her head. "You always say the weirdest things," she muttered, resting her cheek against his shoulder and wrapping her arms around his waist.

"It's a natural talent," Dust retorted teasingly. "Wait for my next show."

Josie leaned back and stared up at Dust with a serious expression. Dust looked down and gave her a crooked smile. He really didn't know what to say.

His eyes widened in surprise when Josie suddenly leaned forward and pressed her lips to his. He started to pull back, but Josie's arms were around his waist preventing him. His hands slid to her hips. He was about to gently push her away when the sound of a throat clearing startled them both apart.

Dust turned his head to see Sammy standing at the corner of the gym. She was staring at him with an uneasy expression. Her gaze moved back and forth between him and Josie several times before she pressed her lips together.

"I thought she was telling you that dinner was ready," Sammy replied in a voice edged with anger. "Neither one of you normally passes up a meal, so I was worried that something bad had happened. Obviously, I was wrong."

"Sammy," Josie started to say.

"I'll talk to her," Dust interjected in a quiet voice.

Josie looked at Dust and flushed. "I shouldn't have…." Her voice died when Dust shook his head.

"Don't feel bad, Josie," Dust muttered, moving from one foot to the other. "It didn't mean anything. You just needed someone and I was here."

Josie nodded. "Yeah, good ole Dust to the rescue again," she muttered, turning on her heel. "Dinner is ready, by the way."

Dust watched Josie walk by Sammy and murmur something softly under her breath. Only when Josie disappeared around the corner did he walk toward Sammy. She was still scowling at him. A slight grin curved the corner of his lips. She would never admit it, but he could tell she was jealous.

"It doesn't feel good, does it?" He asked curiously.

Sammy glared at him and folded her arms across her chest. "What doesn't feel good?" She demanded in a tight voice.

"Feeling jealous," he said, coming to a stop in front of her. "I didn't like it, either."

A frown creased Sammy's brow and the scowl turned to a look of confusion. Dust lifted his hand and ran it along her cheek. She stared warily back at him when he slid his hand down her throat and wrapped it around the back of her neck.

"When did you feel it?" She asked in a slightly husky voice.

Dust took a step closer. "When Randolph was eyeing you," he admitted.

"Randolph?!" Sammy scoffed. "He's a slime bag."

Dust's lips twitched in amusement. "Yeah, he is, but I was still jealous."

"I wouldn't let him kiss me," Sammy whispered, staring into his eyes.

"I'm glad," Dust murmured, pulling Sammy a touch closer. "She's just hurting. She isn't really interested in me."

"I know," Sammy forced out in a barely audible voice. "And yes, she is. Interested… in you, that is."

"Dust! Sammy! Dinner is… Oh," Todd stopped in his tracks and looked back and forth between them with a wide-eyed expression. "Are you kissing again?"

Sammy pulled back and shook her head. "No, we aren't kissing again," she said in a husky voice.

Todd looked at his sister with a doubtful expression. "Are you sure? It sure looked like it," he muttered.

Sammy turned on her heel and reached for her little brother's hand. "I'm sure. Besides, Dust smells like a diesel engine at the moment. Who wants to kiss a motor?" She asked in a teasing tone.

"Is that why you have a black mark on your neck?" Todd asked innocently.

Dust bit back a laugh when Sammy released a soft curse and glanced over her shoulder to glare at him. With a shake of her head, she released Todd's hand and muttered something about needing to go clean up before they ate. Todd giggled and looked back at Dust with a huge, knowing grin.

"She likes you," Todd whispered to Dust as Sammy stomped back into the gym.

"Yeah, well, I like her, too," Dust admitted with a crooked grin. "Tell everyone I'll be there in a minute. I need to get cleaned up first. Someone mentioned that I smelled like an old engine."

"I will. Miss Martha made a big pot of chicken flavored rice and vegetables from the stuff we brought. I didn't even know we had any of it. It smells a lot like what mom used to make," Todd said excitedly before the gleam in his eyes faded a little. "I miss my mom and dad."

"I miss mine, too, Todd," Dust murmured, laying his hand on Todd's thin shoulder. "Go on, I'll be there in a few minutes."

Dust watched Todd turn and walk back toward the entrance of the gym. For a moment, he wished that he had the power to turn back time. Then again, if he could, he'd still need a way to stop the comet and figure out a way to still meet Sammy and Todd. Shaking his head at wishful thoughts, he cleaned up the area before heading through the back door of the gym to the boy's locker room and the bucket of water he had stored in there earlier.

***

Two hours later, Dust sat next to Sammy on one of the mats in the locker room. The others were sitting around it as well. In the center, a fire burned inside the rock circle. It was just enough to keep the chill out of the room.

Raymond had surprised everyone by pulling out a harmonica. He was playing several old tunes, some of which Dust didn't know. Todd was lying with his head on Josie's lap, his eyes growing heavier as the night wore on. What surprised Dust the most was that Denise was sitting close to Randolph. Martha was sitting beside Raymond while Beau was doing a perimeter check.

"That was nice, Raymond," Martha replied when the melody faded. "I never knew you played so well.

I heard you at some of the different functions, but it never dawned on me that you were so good."

Raymond chuckled and gently cleaned the instrument before he wrapped it in the handkerchief and placed it back into his shirt pocket. It was obvious that he cared about the tiny reminder of normal days. For a moment, Dust wished he had some small reminder of his own to carry around with him.

"Being the president of the bank left me little time for my playing. Still, I do enjoy it. I learned how to play when I was about Todd's age," Raymond reminisced. "I begged my father to buy me one. He gave me my first harmonica on my eighth birthday and I've been playing ever since."

"I wish I had learned how to play an instrument," Sammy said with a grin. "I tried out for the band, but I wasn't very good."

"I play the piano," Denise whispered, glancing nervously around. "Not that I could carry that around with me."

"I played the drums for two years," Dust admitted. "I quit when I broke my arm."

Martha chuckled. "I can imagine it would be a little difficult to play one-handed," she replied with a sigh. "I sang in the church choir."

"So did my mom," Josie replied in a soft voice.

"She had a beautiful voice, didn't she, Josie," Randolph said, glancing at his sister. "So do you."

Josie glanced up at her brother in surprise and scowled. "How would you know?" She asked in a clipped tone.

The smile on Randolph's lips faded and a sad look came into them. Dust could tell the other man felt uneasy about conversing with Josie. He watched in surprise when Denise reached over and threaded her fingers through Randolph's in encouragement.

"You used to sing when you hung out at the laundry," Randolph finally said.

"Oh," Josie muttered, falling silent.

"I remember…," Randolph's voice faded and his eyes glazed over as if he was seeing something that wasn't there. "She's coming. I can see her. She isn't far."

"Who?" Raymond asked in surprise.

Randolph blinked several times before he shook his head and looked around at everyone. "The She Devil. She'll be here soon," he choked out.

"We have to get ready," Dust said, rising to his feet. "Raymond, get Beau. Sammy, you have to hide."

Chapter 24

The Battle:

The group rose as one. Even Todd, who had been half asleep, could feel the tension and urgency in the air. They didn't have much time to really get things ready. Between working on the old bus, and Beau and Randolph's arrival, time seemed to be on fast forward.

Dust silently cursed. They had to backtrack and the loss of distance between them and the She Devil was working against them. Still, they had discovered more survivors. Deep down, Dust knew that Raymond, Martha, and Denise wouldn't have lasted very long if they had remained in the town.

"What's your plan?" Beau asked Dust as he stepped into the main area of the gym.

Dust glanced at Josie and Randolph. In reality, they were the only ones that really stood a chance against the creature. Even then, he knew that it wasn't going to be easy. Randolph's main talent lay in knowing when and where the She Devil was. When it came to fighting, it was going to fall on his and Josie's shoulders.

"The She Devil is stronger than she was back at the silo," Dust stated in a quiet voice. "This isn't like the fight back there. This is much, much worse."

Dust watched as Beau paled and swallowed before he gave a sharp nod. Dust didn't miss the quick glance that Beau shot toward Josie before his jaw tightened. Dust could see that Beau realized that he was about to see what Josie could really do. The small flames were nothing compared to what she was capable of creating.

"If you can draw her in, me and the others will blast the hell out of the bitch," Beau said. "The women and the boy need to find a place to hide. Josie can watch over them."

"I see you're still trying to call the shots," Josie muttered under her breath. "If the She Devil is as strong as Dust says she is, then he's going to need my help."

Dust nodded grimly. "She's right, Beau," he said in a slightly hesitant voice. "Raymond can stay with Sammy and the others."

Sammy's lips pursed and she shook her head. "We need a way to draw her out. If she suspects anything, it will be harder to kill her. I think we need to use me as bait. We know that she wants me dead," she suggested in a quiet voice. "Besides, how do you hide from something that can pass through walls? It is better to be out in the open than to hide."

"No, Sammy," Todd cried out in fear, moving closer to his sister so he could wrap his arms around her waist and hold onto her. "I don't want anything to happen to you!"

Sammy's expression softened and she wrapped her arms around Todd and hugged him to her. Her gaze rose and she stared back at Dust. He could see the worry and fear reflected in them, but also the resignation. His gut clenched in response. As much as he hated to admit it, Sammy was right. Even if she hid, the She Devil could find her. Because of that, Sammy would be in more danger than if she was out in the open where they could rally around her.

Dust drew in a deep breath and ran his hand over the back of his neck. His gaze moved around the room. Everyone was staring silently back at him, waiting for him to make a decision. For a moment, he wished he didn't have to be the one to do it. He suddenly felt much older than his fifteen years.

"I hate to admit it, but she's right," Dust replied in a husky voice, turning to look at Martha. "I need you, Denise, and Todd to find a safe place in the locker room. The showers would probably be the safest place," he said before he turned to look at the others. "Beau, you and Raymond set up a perimeter on each side in front of the gym. One can hide behind the remains of the bus shed and the other back behind the concrete sign. Randolph, I want you to stay with Sammy. You can sense where the She Devil is. You let Sammy know if she is near."

"What about me?" Josie asked, rubbing her hands together.

Dust looked at Josie. "You do what you can to protect the others," he said in a quiet voice.

"What are you going to do?" Beau asked in a hard voice.

Dust's lips tightened for a moment before he relaxed them. "I'll be there," he promised. "Get the weapons you'll need. Martha, can you fire a gun?"

Martha nodded her head. "Yes," she said.

"So can I," Denise added softly. "You don't live on a farm and not learn how to."

Dust turned back to Beau. "Make sure they have some weapons," he said, turning away.

"What about me?" Todd asked, looking around at everyone. "What am I supposed to do?"

Dust glanced back at the small, determined face. He saw Sammy's arms tighten protectively around Todd and she gazed back at him with a worried expression. His gaze moved back to Todd and he reached into his pocket and pulled out the pocket knife his dad had given him. He turned back and held it out.

"Take this," he instructed. "Only use it if you have to. I want you to watch Martha and Denise's back."

Todd took the folded blade. He stared down at the small knife in his hand before he looked back up at Dust. A shaky, but brave smile curved his lips.

"I'll watch their back," Todd promised. "Sammy showed me."

* * *

"She's close, maybe a mile or so," Randolph murmured a half hour later.

"Remember, protect Sammy," Dust instructed before he faded.

"Damn," Randolph muttered in a shaky breath. "I don't think I'll ever get used to him doing that."

"It was pretty freaky the first few times," Sammy replied with a shrug. "Now, it seems normal."

"I don't know what normal is anymore," Randolph confessed, staring up at the sky. "It looks like another storm is coming. Maybe she'll seek shelter."

Sammy shook her head and gazed out over the dark gray, rolling clouds. Green lightning flashed in the distance, creating a spider web of light that faded almost as quickly as it appeared. Her fingers tightened around the bow in her left hand. She casually reached up and pulled an arrow out of the sheath strapped to her back.

"She's here," Randolph whispered, staring at the black shape that was slowly moving toward them.

"I see her," Sammy replied, threading the arrow on the string. "Just let me know where she is if she disappears."

Both of them stood waiting as the She Devil swooped down. Their gazes remained locked on her as she landed on the hard packed, dirt parking area in front of the gym. Sammy swallowed. This was not the creature from the silo. This one was different, more evolved. She rose up, over five and a half feet in height, and walked on two legs. Dust hadn't been exaggerating when he said that she had evolved.

The She Devil paused, glancing from side to side with a thoughtful expression. Her long, leathery wings expanded outward for a moment before she folded them around her body like a cape. They were so long that the ends actually dragged along the ground behind her. What fascinated Sammy was that she was wearing clothing that looked almost Grecian in style.

"Where is the one I seek?" The She Devil asked in a slightly husky, accented voice.

Sammy felt Randolph start in surprise. Her left hand clenched the bow tighter while the fingers of her right hand twitched on the long shaft of the arrow in preparation. Drawing in a deep breath, Sammy forced the stiff muscles of her shoulders to relax.

"I'm here," Dust replied, slightly behind the creature. "I don't want to fight you, but I won't let you harm anyone else."

The She Devil partially turned, her dark eyes flowing over Dust. From this angle, Sammy could see that while her face had changed to a more human appearance, her nose and mouth still retained some of the characteristics of her canine DNA. A soft gasp escaped Sammy when the creature's features suddenly distorted. As if in slow motion, the black fur covering her faded and her face and body transformed.

"What the…?," Randolph hissed, staring in disbelief at the human-looking form.

"I have… Evolved, like you," the She Devil whispered to Dust.

"No," Dust replied, staring back at the beautiful creature standing in front of him. "You want to kill. That is not want I want."

The She Devil turned and looked at Sammy and Randolph. Her gaze skimmed over Randolph before she dismissed him. Sammy shivered when the creature's gaze lingered on her.

"I am more powerful than that female," the She Devil stated, turning back to look at Dust. "Join me as my mate. Share your power with me and we will rule this world together."

Dust shook his head again. "No," he said again. "Why do you want me? What power do you think I have?"

The She Devil took a step toward Dust and reached out one slender, delicate hand, as if to touch him. It was enough to make the hair on the back of Sammy's neck stand up in warning. Lifting the bow, she pulled back on the arrow.

"I wouldn't," Sammy warned, staring at the creature.

A soft growl escaped the beast as she turned and hurtled toward Sammy with blinding speed. Sammy released the arrow at the same time as Randolph grabbed her around the waist and twisted with her. The movement knocked them both off balance, and they fell to the ground.

Sammy rolled onto her back and stared up in horror when the creature reappeared where she had been standing. The long shaft of the arrow protruded from the She Devil's right shoulder. A loud snarl escaped the beast when she reached up and snapped the end off.

Sammy and Randolph scooted back several feet before scrambling to their feet. Sammy quickly pulled another arrow from the sheath and threaded it to the string. Her eyes widened in horror when the She Devil reached over her shoulder and pulled the broken shaft through her flesh. Fresh blood, the color of black ink, darkened the white tunic she had wrapped around her. With a flick of her wrist, the beast tossed the broken arrow away from her.

"You will die a slow death, human," the She Devil whispered.

"I'll see you in hell first," Sammy retorted, pulling up the bow again.

The She Devil stared back at Sammy before she threw her head back and laughed. The sound washed over Sammy, sending goose bumps racing across her flesh at the promise held in it. Lightning flashed closer, highlighting the soft mocha skin of the She Devil's shoulders and the quickly healing wound.

The She Devil tilted her head, as if considering Sammy's words. A slow, menacing smile curled her lips, revealing the gleaming white, sharp teeth hidden inside. Sammy stumbled backwards when the creature's face suddenly began to twist.

"I think that can be arranged," the She Devil hissed before returning to her original form.

"Get Sammy out of here," Dust yelled to Randolph.

Sammy lost her grip on the arrow she had threaded when Randolph suddenly twisted and grabbed her arm. She stumbled when he pulled her back toward the gym. Glancing over her shoulder, she saw that Dust had materialized where she was standing just seconds earlier. He was locked in battle with the She Devil.

Chapter 25

Hostage:

Dust strained to hold the She Devil far enough away to keep her snapping jaws from sinking into his flesh. He jerked backwards, fading when she spread her wings and began to lift off the ground. He rolled across the packed gravel and dirt parking lot several feet before he solidified again.

His gaze focused on the female as she rose into the air. Almost immediately, Beau and Raymond began firing at her. A low hissing scream escaped her and she twisted in midair.

Dust followed her gaze. Turning, he took off in the direction of Raymond. He faded, passing through the low concrete wall with the faint words *Springfield High School* on it. Reforming, he opened his arms and tackled Raymond, knocking the older man to the side just as the She Devil struck the concrete.

The concrete exploded outward. Chunks of the flying debris rained down over the two of them. Dazed, Dust shook his head and stared down at Raymond. The other man blinked up at Dust before grunting. Dust glanced over his shoulder. The creature had turned back toward Beau's hiding place.

"Are you okay?" Dust asked in an urgent tone.

"Ye… Yes. Go… Stop her!" Raymond muttered.

Dust pushed up off the ground and turned back to follow the She Devil. He glanced wildly around, trying to sense her movements. He gazed toward Josie. Her hands were glowing and she was turning in a tight circle, looking up at the sky.

"Josie, look out!" Randolph shouted.

Dust watched in horror as Josie's feet were knocked out from under her. Josie rolled to the side, a line of flames shooting out from her hands. Anger swept through Dust when the She Devil briefly appeared. She wrapped her long tail around Josie's ankles and lifted her off the ground.

"Josie!" Beau yelled, aiming his rifle at the creature.

"Shoot it!" Josie screamed, twisting so she could try to hit the creature with a ball of fire.

Dust ran toward Josie, focusing as he did. Small granules of sand began swirling and joining until he felt them wrap around his upper body. Long, gray wings formed and he felt his feet lift off the ground.

The She Devil saw him coming and released Josie. The report of Beau's rifle mixed with Josie's terrified scream. Adrenaline, fueled by anger and fear, pulsed through Dust, and he shot forward, catching Josie a mere foot before she hit the ground.

"I've got this," Josie said breathlessly, clinging to Dust's shoulders. "Let me go."

Dust swept up far enough to drop Josie lightly on her feet. Fury blazed in her eyes and he could see her body beginning to shimmer. Soaring upward, he twisted in time to see the She Devil turn on Beau and

Raymond. Both men were firing at the creature as fast as they could. The bullets flashed through her when she faded, but he could already see that she was beginning to tire.

"She's running out of energy, Josie," Dust shouted.

"I'll show her some energy," Josie growled, her whole body shimmering with intense blue flames. "Let's see how you like to play with fire."

Dust saw Raymond and Beau fall back when Josie's hands shot outward, long whips of brilliant blue flame greedily sped toward the She Devil. The creature turned in the air just as the wall of flames hit her. Her black wings rose up to ward off the incinerating fire Josie was directing at her. Without her wings to support her body in flight, the She Devil fell from the sky. The impact shook the ground with enough force to knock Raymond and Beau off their feet.

Dust slowly lowered himself back to the ground and watched as Josie stalked closer, glowing brighter than he had ever seen. He knew she was using too much energy, but was powerless to tell her to stop. She wouldn't have listened anyway, if he had. She was directing every ounce of her fury at the creature.

The black wings slowly turned a radiant red under the onslaught of the flames. Dust was amazed that the creature hadn't disintegrated into a pile of ash. He stood watching as Josie stopped just a few feet from the creature, her gaze and hands locked on it.

Out of the corner of his eye, he saw Beau and Raymond stagger unsteadily to their feet. Beau glanced at Josie with an expression of awe on his face. Dust started to warn him to stay back when his attention was jerked back to the creature.

A sense of warning struck him a brief second before the She Devil exploded upward. The powerful burst of air from her wings sent a shock wave rippling outward. The impact of it lifted them off their feet, throwing them several yards before they hit the hard surface with a sickening thump. Dust grunted as the breath was momentarily knocked out of him.

He lay on the ground, his ears ringing. With a shake of his head to clear the noise, he pushed up with one hand. Horror gripped him when he saw the She Devil land a couple of feet from where Josie lay helpless, stunned and drained from her assault against the She Devil. His mouth opened in denial when the creature raised her right hand and focused. Five long claws extended outward, growing until they were several inches long.

"No!" Dust mouthed at the same time as he heard Beau's fierce cry.

As if in slow motion, he watched as the She Devil bent to drive the sharp blades of her nails through Josie's chest. The choked cry froze on his lips when he saw Beau fall over Josie at the last second. Beau's ravaged face twisted in shock and disbelief. His arms trembled as he looked down between him and his daughter.

Dust's gaze followed the movement. He could see the tips of the She Devil's claws protruding through the front of Beau's shirt. It was only when the creature pulled back and rose into the air again that Beau's right arm collapsed and he fell to the side.

"NO!" Randolph's harsh cry echoed over the sound of the growing storm. "Dad!"

Dust pushed up off the ground and stumbled over to where Josie and Beau were lying. He watched as Josie rolled and sat up. Her gaze was locked on her father. Dust caught her when she almost fell over trying to get to her knees.

He supported her when she swayed again. "You saved me," Josie whispered in a dazed, confused voice that suddenly sounded very, very young.

Beau was struggling to draw in a breath. Dust could see the bubbles of blood pool up when the man tried to breathe. He knew that the nails had gone through both of Beau's lungs.

"You…," Beau gasped, his eyes growing dim. "Proud… you."

"Daddy," Josie whispered, reaching out to touch his cheek.

"Love… You… Jo…," Beau hissed, his voice fading with the last of his oxygen and strength.

"Dad!" Randolph cried out, falling to his knees on the other side of Beau. "Dad, don't. Help him! You have to help him." Dust looked down at Randolph. The other man's eyes were glazed with grief. "Please, you have to help him."

"He's gone, son," Raymond said, laying his hand on Randolph's shoulder.

Dust felt Josie's shoulders begin to shake and a low anguished sob escaped her. He helped her to her feet and turned her toward him. All he could do was hold her.

"Randolph," Dust murmured. "Where is the She Devil?"

Randolph looked up at Dust and shook his head. "I… I don't know. It was as if a wall was suddenly erected around her," he whispered, his gaze returning to his dad. "One minute she was there, then suddenly she was gone."

***

Fury poured through her as she swept up into the churning night sky. The fact that they were waiting for her had been obvious. How the humans had known of her approach, she didn't know.

She had wanted to kill the one that made fire. Her body throbbed and burned from the combination of assaults. A shuddered escaped her as her body ejected the small pieces of metal from it. Her wings stung and pain coursed through her as new tissue healed over the damaged skin. Her strength was quickly draining away from her and she desperately needed food to restore it, but that would have to wait.

Fading, she circled around and disappeared through the wall of the building. She reformed, landing on the cold concrete in a long room. Lifting her nose, she sniffed the air. Three separate scents swept through her.

Her gaze swept over the dark area. A low fire burned in the center of a group of rocks. Stepping on silent feet, she shifted into her human-like form. Bending, she picked up one of the blankets off a padded cushion and wrapped it around her body just as one of the human's that she scented glanced around the corner where they were hiding. A startled cry escaped the older woman and she froze in uncertainty.

"Who are you?" The woman demanded in confusion. "Where did you come from?"

The She Devil tilted her head and took a step closer. "Where is the one called Sammy?" She asked in a husky voice.

"Sammy?" The woman said, taking a step closer. "She's with Dust and the others. I thought I heard shouting. I thought they were fighting the She Devil."

"They… were," the She Devil whispered, stopping in front of the woman.

"Who are you?" The woman asked again, this time unable to keep the tremor out of her voice.

The She Devil flashed her sharp teeth. "The She Devil," she replied. She reached out and grabbed the woman's hand holding the weapon in her right hand and the woman's neck with her left. "Where is the smaller male who travels with the one called Sammy?"

"Never!" The woman started to choke out.

"Martha?" Another voice called out from the darkness.

Turning her gaze toward the back, she caught a glimpse of another human female and the male that she was seeking. A soft snarl escaped her when she saw the human raise the weapon in her hand. Her eyes narrowed and she tossed the old woman she was holding to the side, ignoring the woman when her head hit the wall and she collapsed to the floor.

"Martha! Stop! I don't know who you are, but stay back!" The young human female warned, her hand shaking as the She Devil walked toward her.

"Step aside human and I will not kill you. I need you to give the one named Dust a message for me," the She Devil hissed.

"N… No, stay back… back," the woman whispered.

"Denise, it's her. Look at her eyes. It's the She Devil. Shoot her," the boy warned in a voice filled with fear. "Shoot her!"

"You are smart, young one," The She Devil chuckled, walking toward them. "Unfortunately, the hot lead from your weapons cannot kill me. You, female, tell Dust to bring me the one called Sammy and I may let the boy child live."

"No!" Denise cried as her finger squeezed the trigger.

The She Devil knew that time was running out. In the distance, she could hear the others. She was too low on energy to battle again. A low, feral snarl escaped her and she shifted. Charging toward the female, she twisted in mid-flight. The hot lead from the girl's weapon flashed by her. Her arm swept out, throwing the woman to the side even as her other arm wrapped around the terrified boy.

"Let me go!" He cried, straining to break free. "Sammy! Dust!"

"Not yet, young one," The She Devil responded in a cold voice. "This time, *I* will be the one to set the trap."

She burst out through the double doors in the back of the room, snapping the thick chain wrapped around the door handles like it was a piece of string. Unfolding her wings, she tucked the struggling body of the boy against her and launched upward.

Long fragmented lines of lightning crisscrossed the sky. The wind was picking up as the storm grew closer. It was both a blessing and a curse. It would give her the time she needed to gather her strength for the upcoming battle that was imminent, but it would also drain even more of her energy as she flew back to her temporary lair.

"Sammy!" The boy cried pitifully against her chest.

"Soon, human. Soon, she and Dust will come for you and when they do, this world will see a new species, unlike anything they have seen before," The She Devil replied with satisfaction. "Soon."

***

Sammy's gaze remained glued to the scene unfolding outside the window. She watched the fight between the She Devil and her friends. Her hand rose and she pressed her fist tightly to her mouth to smother her cry of fear when she saw the She Devil lift Josie up by her ankles.

A part of her wanted to argue with Randolph when he insisted that they find shelter back inside the gym. She hadn't wanted to go, but she knew that if she stayed outside it would make it more difficult for Dust, Josie, and the two men to focus on killing the creature. She knew deep down that if she had stayed, they would have been focusing on trying to keep her safe instead.

Even so, she and Randolph couldn't completely desert the others. They had sought refuge in the ticket booth. They watched the fight outside through the narrow window.

"I can't believe that she looks human," Randolph muttered. "How the hell is that possible?"

"I don't know how she did it," Sammy whispered, staring in horror at the fight. "Look at Josie. I've never seen her glow so bright before."

"Holy crud!" Randolph choked out in disbelief. "They are both a lot more powerful than we thought."

"Yes, they are… What's going on? Oh, no!" Sammy cried a moment before both of them were thrown back against the far wall when a blast of heated air hit them.

The thick glass of the ticket booth cracked, leaving a spider web of jagged lines splintering outward.

Sammy groaned and touched the back of her head where it had connected with the wall. Randolph was pushing up off the floor. He had landed under the small counter a few feet from her.

"What happened?" He muttered, shaking his head.

Sammy shook her head and winced. "I don't know," she replied.

They both rose on shaky feet and made their way over to the fragmented window. Horror gripped them both when they saw the distorted image of the She Devil standing over Josie's still figure.

"No!" They both cried out at the same time.

As if in slow motion, they saw the She Devil bend forward, her long nails extended. Just before she drove them downward, Beau appeared. Randolph's choked denial resonated through the small room and his body jerked in time with his father as the She Devil drove her nails through Beau's body.

"Dad!" Randolph mumbled in disbelief, pulling back and turning toward the door.

"Randolph, no!" Sammy yelled, trying to stop him.

Sammy followed, pausing at the entrance to the gym. She watched as Randolph ran across the front parking area. Her gaze moved to the She Devil as she rose into the air. Her fingers curled and she wished she had her bow. It was still in the ticket booth.

Turning, Sammy returned to the small room. She hurried over to where she had dropped her bow and quiver of arrows. Grief and anger filled her. As much as she hated what Beau and Randolph had done, the death of another human was just a re-enforcement that they were living in a different world than before the comet.

Brushing her hair away from her face, she started to turn toward the front of the gym when the sound of gunfire from the locker room drew her attention. Her eyes widened in fear and she turned in the direction of the noise. The sound of a soft snarl sent a shaft of terror through her.

"Please, no!" Sammy whispered, taking off at a run through the gym. "Please, oh, please, no!"

Sammy burst through the doorway of the locker room. Her gaze swept wildly around the area before locking on where Denise was helping Martha sit up. Sammy started forward, her gaze searching.

"Where's Todd?" She demanded in a hoarse voice. "Denise, where is my brother?"

Denise looked up at Sammy with dazed eyes. She shook her head. Martha raised a shaky hand to her bleeding temple.

"She took him," Denise whispered, her eyes filling with tears. "She said to tell Dust to bring you to her and she might let Todd live. I'm sorry, Sammy. I tried to stop her, but she was too fast. She looked… She looked human, too."

Sammy stumbled back a step before she turned. They had to go after the She Devil. They had to stop her before she hurt Todd. A gut-wrenching terror filled Sammy. She needed Dust's help.

***

Dust stared down at Beau's still, blood-covered body. Despair threatened to choke him. For a moment, he thought of all the things he might have done to prevent this from happening. The She Devil had taken him by surprise. When she had transformed into a shape that was more human, he found himself having doubts about whether he should destroy her. It was one thing to kill a deranged animal, but to kill something that looked like a human…. Deep down, guilt rose up. He should have done more to protect the others. He should have confronted the She Devil on his own.

"Dust!" Sammy cried out, emerging from the gym.

Dust turned, his arms still supporting Josie's trembling form. Sammy was running toward him. Fear, horror, and despair was reflected in her eyes. His gaze moved to where Martha and Denise emerged from the gym. Denise was holding Martha around the waist. The older woman had blood running from her temple.

"Where's Todd?" Dust asked, turning his gaze back to Sammy. "Sammy, where's Todd?"

"She took him," Sammy sobbed, wiping her arm across her face. "The She Devil took him."

***

"You've got to connect with her again, Randolph," Dust murmured under his breath almost two hours later.

"I'm trying," Randolph muttered, tiredly rubbing his forehead. "I don't know if it is the storm or what, but all I'm getting is a blank wall."

Dust released his breath and rose to his feet. "Keep trying," he said, turning away.

"Dust," Randolph called quietly.

Dust turned and glanced down at Randolph where he sat on the bottom bleacher near the door of the gym. He could see the shock and grief still mirrored in Randolph's eyes. Dust felt sorry for Randolph and Josie. While he couldn't say he had liked Beau, he wouldn't have wanted the old man dead either.

"Yeah?" Dust asked, thrusting his hands in the front pockets of his jeans.

"Thank you… For giving dad a proper burial," Randolph said before he turned back around and closed his eyes.

Dust turned back and began walking along the bleachers to the end. His mind kept replaying the scene from earlier as he silently climbed back down and headed toward the locker room. He kept trying to think if there could have been some way he could have prevented Beau from being killed. Drawing in a deep breath, he thought of the short funeral they had given Beau. At least, they had been able to give Josie and Randolph that simple ceremony to help with their grief, and hopefully give them a semblance of closure.

***

Dust tiredly rubbed his forehead. Shortly after the battle, he and Randolph had wrapped Beau's body in an old furniture blanket that Raymond had found in one of the storage closets. There hadn't been much time to say goodbye. The storm had grown closer and more intense. Sammy held Josie up while Denise stood next to Randolph. Raymond held Martha. Each person said a quiet goodbye before Dust knelt and touched the ground, opening it just far enough for Beau's body to disappear before resealing it again.

He watched as everyone but Sammy and Josie turned and slowly walked back to the shelter of the gym. Walking over to the two girls standing silently nearby, he stepped between them and wrapped an arm around each one of them in support. Sammy leaned her head against his shoulder while Josie stood stiff, a small part of her closed off.

"Why does the world have to be so heartbreaking?" Sammy whispered, staring down at the fresh grave.

"I don't know," Dust murmured, staring out at the approaching storm. "If I could shield you two from it, I would."

"Well, you can't," Josie replied bitterly, raising a hand to wipe at a tear. "You can't make the world a better place. It just keeps getting crappier."

"We can try, Josie," Dust said, sliding his arm from around her to hold her hand. "Together, we can make wherever we are a little better, brighter, than it was."

Josie pulled away from Dust, staring at him and Sammy with a twisted expression of grief and anger. She opened her mouth to say something before she closed it. Shaking her head, she turned toward the gym.

"I need food," she said.

"You're hungry?" Sammy asked in astonishment.

Josie shook her head again and stared at them with hard, cold eyes. "No, but if we are going after Todd, I'm going to make sure that I'm fully charged. No one messes with my little man and gets away with it. I'm pissed, and the next time I meet that hairy-assed bitch, I'm going to drop a fire bomb down her throat."

Dust winced when pea-sized hail began to fall. He raised his hand, forming a shield around them without thinking. Together, they hurried back inside the building.

Dust thought of Josie's vow to get Todd back. Deep down, he hoped that they could. He knew one thing; he would do everything he could to bring the little boy safely home or die trying.

..*

Pulling his thoughts back to the present, he was almost back to the locker room where the others were sitting, when he felt the first thread of connection. Stopping in the short corridor, he pressed his back against the wall and closed his eyes. His heart raced before slowing as the image grew clearer.

A few miles from the gym was an old building. It looked like it was a grain processing plant or something. Dust was staring up at the roof. Rain poured through the opening where part of the metal had been torn back by the weather.

He slowly looked down at the body he was in. It was the She Devil. She had changed back to her more 'human' form. In the background, he heard a slight shuffle. Turning, he saw Todd sitting in the corner.

"Why are you doing this?" Todd asked in a trembling voice. "Why do you want to hurt us? We haven't done nothing to you."

Dust's heart ached for the frightened, but courageous little boy. He was so much like Sammy, that Dust couldn't help but wonder what he would be like when he grew up. Refocusing on the scene in front of him, Dust waited for the She Devil to respond.

"You ask why I seek power," the She Devil said, walking over to stand in front of Todd. "I was once like you, small and weak. My brothers and sisters pushed me out into the storm, uncaring of my fate."

"You've got brothers and sisters, too?" Todd whispered in awe.

The She Devil's soft chuckle filled the small area that was once an office. She reached out and lifted Todd's chin. Dust could feel Todd's reaction, but the

She Devil tightened her grip until the little boy whimpered in pain.

"Had," she murmured, releasing Todd's chin. "I killed them and the bitch that had me. I was hungry, ravenous for food. I discovered the more I ate, the more powerful I became and I began to… Change."

"You mean like Dust and Josie?" Todd asked innocently.

The She Devil looked thoughtful before she turned away to stare out the door again. Dust could feel the cold metal from the frame between his palm and clenched his fists. He had to remain silent so that the beast wasn't aware of him inside her.

"Not like the female that makes fire, though she is interesting," the She Devil murmured. "No, I am more like the one called Dust. He continues to evolve like me. Together, we will make a new species." She turned to look at Todd again. "A species that will rule this new world."

"But… Why do you want to hurt Sammy? She doesn't want to hurt you," Todd insisted.

The She Devil snorted and turned away again. "She stands in my way," she whispered. "She has your heart. Do you think I do not know that you are inside me, Dust? Do you think I can not feel your presence? Come for the boy, but bring me the one called Sammy. I will spare the boy in return for her life… And your promise to stay by my side. Come to me or you will feel every slice I make into the young human's body as if you were doing it."

Dust jerked, opening his eyes and pulling away. He stared into Sammy's worried ones. Her lips were slightly parted and her eyes were wide with horror. It was then that he realized that he had spoken the words of the She Devil aloud, as if they were coming from him.

"Don't let her," Sammy whispered. "Please, Dust, don't… Don't let her kill him, too."

Chapter 26

Evolution:

Dust stared out the window of the old bus. He had wanted to come alone, but both Sammy and Josie had threatened him. Fear twisted his gut and he glanced over at Sammy sitting across from him. She turned her head to stare back at him, a faint smile curved her lips even though it didn't reach her eyes.

"You should have stayed back at the gym," Dust muttered, his voice barely loud enough to be heard over the sound of the engine.

"You are beginning to sound like a broken record," Sammy replied, turning to look out of the window. "The storm clouds are building again."

"Yeah, I saw that," Dust said, sliding across the aisle to sit next to Sammy. "We'll pull up here," he called out to Josie.

"'Kay," Josie replied, pulling off the road onto the median. "So, is that the place?" Josie asked, turning off the engine.

"Yeah," Dust said, sliding out of the seat to stand up next to Josie. "Remember the plan."

"I know," Josie retorted. "You and Sammy keep the She Devil distracted while I sneak in and rescue Todd. I get him away, then I launch a fireball to let you know that we are clear. In the meantime, you guys keep her distracted without getting killed. Once

Todd is hidden away, I come back and help you defeat the bitch while Sammy takes Todd and runs."

"Something like that," Dust retorted with a shake of his head and opened the door of the bus. "We'll drive slow to give you time to get there."

"Thanks. I just hope the storm holds off until this is over," Josie replied with a sigh.

"Me, too," Sammy said, pulling the strap of the quiver holding her arrows over her shoulder before she flipped her ponytail back out of the way. "Be safe, Josie."

Josie paused as she started down the steps. A wry smile curved her lips. She stared back at Sammy for a brief second before she shook her head and stared out the door.

"I'll bring Little Man back safe, don't you worry, Sammy," Josie replied in a soft voice before she disappeared out the door.

Dust and Sammy watched as Josie took off across the uneven ground at a steady jog. They waited in silence until she disappeared. Dust leaned forward and grabbed the lever for the door and closed it again.

"I hope the storm holds off," Sammy said softly, glancing up at the strange, swirling clouds. "I don't like the feel of this one. There's something weird about it."

"Yeah, I feel it, too," Dust muttered. "You'd better sit back down. The road isn't in very good shape off of the main highway."

Dust started the bus and put it into gear. Releasing the brake, he gave the old bus enough gas to get it rolling. His gaze kept moving to the clouds. Sammy was right, there was just something weird about them today.

***

Josie breathed deeply to calm her pounding heart. Her gaze swept over the building. It looked more like a death trap. Large sections of the processing plant were lying like twisted skeletons on the ground, with long pieces of metal sticking upward.

She scanned the area thoroughly before she ran to the next section of debris. Dust had drawn, from his vision last night, a rough sketch of the processing plant interior. Josie just hoped it was accurate. If it was, Todd would be on the second floor in the main section where most of the windows were missing.

Jogging over to the side of the building, Josie glanced up at the second floor. She walked along the side, keeping a metal walkway between her and the second floor windows just in case the creature decided to take a peek out. Her head turned when she heard the loud sound of the school bus and the flash of the headlights in the dim light of the afternoon.

"Time to climb," she whispered, grabbing hold of a drainage pipe connected to the corner of the building.

She tested it before she began climbing. Her head turned when she heard the bus stop. From this angle, she could see Dust through the windshield. She paused until she saw him rise out of the seat.

Gripping the metal railing of the walkway, Josie gingerly pressed her foot to it while still holding onto the pipe. Reassured that it would hold her weight, she nimbly climbed over the railing and pressed her back against the building.

"She Devil," Sammy yelled. "I want my brother back!"

Josie bit back a laugh. *If that didn't get the bitch's attention, nothing would,* she thought.

Peering through one of the broken windows, Josie decided it would be better to be inside than out on the walkway like a duck on the Duck Shoot at the local fair. She glanced inside and noted where the glass was before she climbed through the window.

Now, to find Todd, she thought as she moved through the first room.

..*

Dust winced when Sammy yelled out. He knew it was part of the plan, but he suddenly wished they had thought of a better one. He definitely didn't like the fact that Sammy was standing out in the open.

Sammy stood with her feet apart, her bow gripped tightly in her left hand and an arrow in her right. The wind swirled around them, stirring up the dirt and sending icy chills down the collar of their jackets.

"She Devil!" Sammy yelled again. "You want me, you come and get me, but I want my brother first!"

Dust's gaze narrowed when the creature stepped out of the shadows of the warehouse. She was dressed once again in a sheet wrapped around her like an ancient toga. A shiver ran through Dust when the creature's gaze moved down over Sammy with a slightly triumphant glare.

"Where's my brother?" Sammy demanded, threading the arrow and lifting it to aim at the She Devil.

The creature paused and tilted her head. Dust took a step closer to Sammy. His fists clenched in anticipation.

"I see why you enjoy him," the She Devil finally responded. "He is amusing."

"Where is he?" Sammy asked through clenched teeth. "If you've harmed one hair on his head, I'll kill you."

A delicate laugh escaped the creature and she smiled, showing off her sharp teeth. "You have no powers, yet you threaten me. You are like the others of your species. You act fierce, but in reality you humans are weak. The men screamed and tried to fight me when I came to them, yet they were helpless."

"I'm the one you want," Dust interjected in a quiet voice. "Release the boy and let him and Sammy leave. This is between us. Leave them and the others alone."

The She Devil shook her head. "As long as she lives, you will never really be mine. You may take the boy to the others in your pack, but the girl is mine in return. Then, you will come to me," she stated with a wave of her hand.

Dust's shook his head. "I can't do that," he replied when he saw a brilliant flash of light in the sky behind the warehouse. He turned his gaze back to the She Devil. "Sammy, get out of here."

..*

Sammy nodded and started backwards, keeping her gaze and the arrow on the She Devil. She had seen Josie's signal as well. The soft growl of the beast caused her to pause, but only for a moment. Turning on her heel, she ran for the bus when the warehouse behind the She Devil suddenly exploded into flames.

Rage flared in the creature's eyes and she snarled. Her face twisted, changing as her body shifted. The loose fitting tunic ripped as she continued to grow in size. Sammy watched in horror as the She Devil mutated into a far different beast from even the night before. Her legs lengthened and hair grew along her body. Her nose grew into a long muzzle and her sharp teeth became even longer.

"Oh, my god," Sammy whispered as she slid into the driver's seat of the bus. Her fingers fumbled for the key. She turned it to the on position, waiting impatiently for the light on the dash to go out so she could start it. "Come on!"

A startled scream escaped her when the creature howled loudly. Sammy twisted the key and pressed on the gas. Gripping the shifter, she pulled it down into reverse and pressed her foot down as far as she could. The She Devil had evolved again – this time into a werewolf.

* * *

Dust could feel the change sweeping over the She Devil. He felt his own body reacting to the danger. For a moment, it felt like he was trapped inside himself, struggling to get out. Saliva flooded his mouth and when he tried to swallow it, his tongue brushed against the back of his teeth. That wouldn't have been a problem if it wasn't for the fact that his canines felt strange, longer than normal.

His vision suddenly cleared and he swore it was sharper than before. He could see the pulsing vein in the She Devil's throat. The sound of her heart beat like a drum in his head. Dust backed up, staring through the doors of the burning building. He could see a figure emerge from it. Behind him, he could hear the grinding gears of the bus as Sammy sped away. All of this he was able to process within seconds.

"What's happening to us?" Dust choked out, staring at the large fur-coated beast in front of him.

The She Devil snarled at him. Dust felt sure that she would attack, but instead, she turned and headed straight for Josie. A dark rage hit Dust hard and he moved. One second he was behind the beast, the next he was in front, forcing her to fall back.

"Uh-oh," Josie whispered, the flames lighting her body up. "Dust?"

"This is between us, Josie," Dust growled, staring at the She Devil as she paced back and forth. "Go find

Sammy and Todd. Make sure they get back to the gym safely."

"Okay," Josie muttered, eyeing Dust and the She Devil with wide, wary eyes. "Are you... Are you sure?"

"Get out of here, Josie," Dust snapped, his eyes blazing a dark red.

Dust turned, circling the She Devil when she snapped at Josie. A hiss escaped him when the She Devil lunged, trying to get past him. He threw up his arm, blocking her from getting past him.

"I told you that this was between us now," Dust warned.

You should have joined me, the She Devil snarled. *Now, we are mortal enemies. If you had joined me, we could have ruled this world.*

"I never wanted to rule the world," Dust responded in a quiet voice.

The power was ours, she growled.

"The power should be used to make this a better place," Dust argued, circling around the She Devil.

There will be others like me. I will create them and we will rule, she hissed in anger. *I wanted you to rule by my side. Our two powers could have forged a greater one.*

Dust paused and shook his head. "We have evolved, Daciana," he whispered, the name for her whispering through his mind like a ghostly figure. He didn't know how he knew that is what she would come to be called, but the name fit her. "What we make of our species will be up to us."

The She Devil slowly shifted, her face and body twisting and pulling back into itself as she became more human-like. She stared back at Dust with dark, distrustful eyes. Dust kept his gaze locked on her face, waiting for her response.

"Daciana. I like that," she finally murmured, staring back at him. "You know that this is just the beginning, Dust. We will meet again," she stated more than asked.

"Yes, I know," Dust said, taking a step back.

"The female, she will not accept what you have become," Daciana sneered.

Dust hid his feelings of unease. He knew that Sammy might not accept him now. But, they were both still young. He would worry about her accepting him when they were older. Right now, they were still just learning how to survive.

"I won't let you kill other survivors," Dust warned. "I'll hunt you down if you do. I mean it."

Daciana flashed her teeth at him and stepped back. She rolled her shoulders before she glanced up at the strange, swirling clouds. Time would tell who would evolve to be the most powerful of the two new species – the Lycan or the….

"Until we meet again, Dust," Daciana chuckled. "It will be interesting to see how long you can resist killing your own kind."

Dust didn't say anything. He watched as Daciana shifted again. Her dark brown and black fur appeared to glow against the dying fire. Dust's gaze followed her as she took off at a run, disappearing into the growing darkness.

He stood there for a long, long time before he turned back in the direction of the gym. For a moment, he thought about what Daciana said. She was right. He wasn’t sure how long it would be before his hunger made it impossible for him to resist turning on those that he cared about. Bowing his head, he breathed deeply as an agonizing pain washed through him. He couldn't go back. He would never risk endangering Sammy, Todd, or the others.

Looking up at the sky, he released a cry that shook the surrounding area. Already he could feel the need to hunt burning inside him. The hunger gnawing at his gut. Taking off at a run, he focused. Long wings formed behind him. This time, they were not made of sand, but from his very thoughts. He swept up into the sky, heading away from the old gym and the only family he had.

Chapter 27

Hope:

Dust slowly withdrew his teeth from the small rabbit he held. He stroked the trembling creature and murmured a few soft, reassuring words before he lowered it to the ground. With a thought, he released it from his hold. Almost immediately, it took off.

He watched it disappear back down the hole that he had coaxed it and three others out of. He made sure to take just enough to keep his hunger at bay. It was a constant search, but over the last few weeks, he had learned how to control his hunger. With a sigh, he turned back toward the highway. He would need to find a place to rest before long.

In the distance, he could hear the familiar sound of a diesel engine approaching. His head tilted and he listened. One of the cylinders had a slight miss in it. Hope filled him and his lips curled upward when he heard Randolph and Josie's familiar voices above the roar of it.

..*

"There!" Randolph said, pointing. "I told you I could find him!

"I admit I had my doubts," Josie retorted, drawing laughter from the small group riding in the short, faded yellow bus.

Josie winced when the brakes squealed loudly as they pulled alongside the solitary figure walking along the highway. She pulled the door open and glanced down through the opening. A crooked, somewhat sarcastic grin curved her lips.

"We have room for one more if you need a lift," she called down.

"I'm good," Dust replied.

"Yeah, well, I'm sure the hell not," Josie retorted. "Do you have any idea how many back roads and potholes I've driven over the last three weeks? I'm surprised this thing is still running. Besides, we could always use a good mechanic on board. Raymond and Randolph don't know shit about working on engines."

"Ha-ha, Josie," Randolph replied from behind her. "I don't see you fighting us to get under the hood."

Dust stopped in his tracks and released a deep sigh when the bus rolled to a stop beside him and Josie shut off the engine. He still didn't look at her, or any of the others. He could feel their eyes on him as they hung out of the windows. One pair in particular pulled at him to turn around and look.

Instead, he forced himself to stare straight ahead down the road. Deep down, he was afraid – almost terrified – that this wasn't real. What if some bizarre part of his imagination had created an illusion of them being there?

"Dust," Sammy's soft voice called.

He slowly turned when he heard Sammy's husky voice. A soft groan escaped him when he saw her staring back at him from the steps of the bus. He stumbled backwards when she jumped down onto the road just a few feet from him.

Drawing in a deep breath, he started to lower his head when his gaze locked on the small box in her hands. It was wrapped in the comic strips from an old newspaper. A bow made of string hung limply from the top of it.

"What's that?" He asked in a husky voice.

"It's your birthday present," Sammy whispered, holding it out. "You weren't there, so we had to come find you."

Dust swallowed and reached for the box. His fingers trembled when they brushed against her knuckles. He gripped the package and pulled it close to him, blinking back the tears burning his eyes.

"What is it?" He asked, shaking it gently.

"Open it," Sammy said with a nervous giggle. "We all kind of worked together to make it. It isn't much."

Dust glanced up. His gaze ran along the line of faces staring back at him. He could feel his cheeks flush at their encouraging smiles. Looking back down at the package, he carefully pulled the paper back. He glanced back up at Sammy. She bit her bottom lip and stared back at him with a quiet intensity that made him nervous.

He pulled the lid off. Inside was a colorful necklace. It looked like glass, but it was unlike anything he had ever seen before. Each tiny section was a different color, but they were all fused together. A dark piece of string made up the chain.

"The green one is mine," Todd called out from the front window. "I found it."

"I like the brown one. It reminded me of your eyes," Sammy added in a soft voice. "Josie melted them all together. Denise did the design."

"Raymond and I found the silver. We figured you could use it if you ever meet the She Devil again," Randolph said.

Dust's gaze flashed to Josie. She was leaning against the steering wheel grinning down at him. He saw her give a small shrug.

"We missed you," Sammy said.

Dust jumped when he felt her warm hand against his chilled skin. He looked back at her in confusion, unsure of what to say. His gaze ran over all the faces again before it returned to Sammy.

"Sammy, I don't think," he started to say.

He swallowed when she lifted her hand and gently placed her fingers against his lips to silence him. She had that fierce, determined expression on her face again. The one he had come to love.

"Then, don't," she said. "You are a part of this family. We love you."

"There's something you should know," Dust muttered against her fingers.

"Josie already told us. She sort of guessed when your teeth did the, you know...." She wiggled her fingers in a downward movement. "We'll figure it out in time," Sammy promised with a small smile.

"Okay," Dust replied.

He released the breath he was holding when Sammy suddenly wrapped her arms around his neck and hugged him close. He could feel her hot breath and warm tears against his neck. Her body trembled. His arms moved instinctively around her waist and he pulled her close.

"Happy birthday, Dust," she sniffed. "I really missed you."

"Thanks, Sammy," Dust replied. "Thanks for finding me."

"Always," she whispered, leaning back and pressing a kiss against his lips.

"Aw, man, they're kissing again," Todd said in disgust, sitting back in his seat. "I thought vampires just drank people's blood."

Josie's laughter drown out the muttered hushing the others were trying to do. "Come on, you two. This circus has a long way to go if we are going to try to find your relatives, Dust. We're running short on gas, short on food, and I think we might just get some snow tonight."

"That's okay," Dust retorted as he climbed up the steps into the bus. "I know someone who loves to play with fire."

Dust sent a crooked grin to everyone as he made his way to the back of the bus with Sammy. He didn't have much choice considering she still had a death grip on his hand. He slid into the seat next to her, grinning when Todd quickly changed to the seat in front of them and turned to stare at him with wide eyes filled with awe.

"So, can you do any really cool stuff as a vampire?" Todd asked, resting his chin on the seat as Josie pulled away.

"Yeah, I can do some really cool things now," Dust replied with a smile, holding onto Sammy's hand.

He listened as the others talked back and forth to each other. For a moment, his gaze shifted back to the darkness outside. He'd had a lot of time to think over the last three weeks. This world was a lot different than it had been two years before. He was a lot different. Every day was a new one and you never knew how it might end. The only thing you could do was make the best of it, try to make the world a better place, and hope that you got a chance to try again tomorrow.

"Happy birthday, Dust," he murmured.

If you loved this story by me (S. E. Smith) please leave a review. You can also take a look at additional books and sign up for my newsletter at http://sesmithfl.com **and** http://sesmithya.com to hear about my latest releases or keep in touch using the following links:

Website: http://sesmithfl.com
Newsletter: http://sesmithfl.com/?s=newsletter
Facebook: https://www.facebook.com/se.smith.5
Twitter: https://twitter.com/sesmithfl
Pinterest: http://www.pinterest.com/sesmithfl/
Blog: http://sesmithfl.com/blog/
Forum: http://www.sesmithromance.com/forum/

Additional Books by S.E. Smith

YA Books

Voyage of the Defiance: Breaking Free series
Dust: Before and After

Paranormal and Science Fiction short stories and novellas

For the Love of Tia (Dragon Lords of Valdier Book 4.1)

A Dragonlings' Easter (Dragonlings of Valdier Book 1.1)

A Dragonlings' Haunted Halloween (Dragonlings of Valdier Book 1.2)

A Dragonlings' Magical Christmas (Dragonlings of Valdier Book 1.3)

A Warrior's Heart (Marastin Dow Warriors Book 1.1)

Rescuing Mattie (Lords of Kassis: Book 3.1)

Science Fiction/Paranormal Novels

Cosmos' Gateway Series

Tink's Neverland (Cosmo's Gateway: Book 1)
Hannah's Warrior (Cosmos' Gateway: Book 2)
Tansy's Titan (Cosmos' Gateway: Book 3)
Cosmos' Promise (Cosmos' Gateway: Book 4)
Merrick's Maiden (Cosmos' Gateway Book 5)

Curizan Warrior

Ha'ven's Song (Curizan Warrior: Book 1)

Dragon Lords of Valdier

Abducting Abby (Dragon Lords of Valdier: Book 1)
Capturing Cara (Dragon Lords of Valdier: Book 2)
Tracking Trisha (Dragon Lords of Valdier: Book 3)
Ambushing Ariel (Dragon Lords of Valdier: Book 4)
Cornering Carmen (Dragon Lords of Valdier: Book 5)
Paul's Pursuit (Dragon Lords of Valdier: Book 6)
Twin Dragons (Dragon Lords of Valdier: Book 7)

Lords of Kassis Series

River's Run (Lords of Kassis: Book 1)
Star's Storm (Lords of Kassis: Book 2)
Jo's Journey (Lords of Kassis: Book 3)
Ristéard's Unwilling Empress (Lords of Kassis: Book 4)

Magic, New Mexico Series

Touch of Frost (Magic, New Mexico Book 1)
Taking on Tory (Magic, New Mexico Book 2)

Sarafin Warriors

Choosing Riley (Sarafin Warriors: Book 1)
Viper's Defiant Mate (Sarafin Warriors Book 2)

The Alliance Series
Hunter's Claim (The Alliance: Book 1)
Razor's Traitorous Heart (The Alliance: Book 2)
Dagger's Hope (The Alliance: Book 3)
Zion Warriors Series
Gracie's Touch (Zion Warriors: Book 1)
Krac's Firebrand (Zion Warriors: Book 2)
Paranormal and Time Travel Novels
Spirit Pass Series
Indiana Wild (Spirit Pass: Book 1)
Spirit Warrior (Spirit Pass Book 2)
Second Chance Series
Lily's Cowboys (Second Chance: Book 1)
Touching Rune (Second Chance: Book 2)

Excerpts of S. E. Smith Books

If you would like to read more S. E. Smith stories, she recommends Abducting Abby, the first in her Dragon Lords of Valdier Series. Or if you prefer a Paranormal or Time Travel with a twist, you can check out Lily's Cowboys or Indiana Wild…

About S. E. Smith

S.E. Smith is a ***New York Times, USA TODAY, International, and Award-Winning*** Bestselling author of science fiction, fantasy, paranormal, and contemporary works for adults, young adults, and children. She enjoys writing a wide variety of genres that pull her readers into worlds that take them away.

CPSIA information can be obtained
at www.ICGtesting.com
Printed in the USA
LVOW12s1847220616
493671LV00018B/949/P

9 781942 562849